REUNION AT THUNDER LAKE

Vacation Romance

By Carolyn R. Scheidies

C_R Publications

Carolyn R. Scheidies
415 E 15th
Kearney, NE 68847-6959
(308) 234-3849
crscheidies@hotmail.com Subject Line:
Hope

I DEAL IN HOPE
http://IDealinHope.com

Second Print Edition 2015
ISBN 978-0-6151-6085-6

First Kindle Edition 2015

PROLOGUE

My son, forget not my law; but let thine heart keep my commandments: for length of days, and long life, and peace, shall they add to thee. Proverbs 3:1-2

Mark surveyed the sleek woman striding toward him. Her face set with purpose, she held the bundle of receiving blankets carefully away from her bright red designer dress. His heart tripped as it had the first time his gorgeous wife walked into his life five years ago. Maybe, maybe the precious treasure she carried would change her mind.

Vanessa had not changed since that night when he fell in love with her. She still moved with the grace of a model, while retaining the curves of a movie star. Back then, Mark thought he was dreaming when she turned her green eyes his way. Not given to arrogance about his looks, Mark did not see what she saw in him--a tall, broad shouldered, ruggedly handsome individual with both the intelligence and a desire to succeed.

Five years earlier, the ambitious socialite hitched herself to the up-and-coming handsome young lawyer. However, the face she now turned toward him was cold and petulant. "Here," she shoved the bundle toward him so abruptly he grabbed it, grasping it to his chest as a tiny cry of distress emanated from the bundle.

"Venee," he started.

"Don't call me that. I hate that name." Absently she patted her perfectly coiffured hair. Diamond earrings twinkled in the light.

"Won't you reconsider? We can work things out, I know we can. With God's help..."

The graceful woman jerked. "God? If it weren't for your concern for your religion, we wouldn't be in this mess."

"Venee. Sorry. I mean, there has to be a way." His shoulders tensed as she surveyed him coldly.

"Once, maybe, if you had not given up your opportunity to practice with father's prestigious New York law firm to live in some God-forsaken small Midwest town. I thought I married a lawyer, not some small-town businessman. Really, running a *Christian* book store?"

"Not God-forsaken," Mark corrected gently. "Listen. Please listen. We have more than ourselves to consider." He tried not to panic. "We are a family now. The Midwest is a great place to raise a family."

"No." She cut him off sharply. "You have that to consider, not me. Not now, not ever. At least, not with this or with you." She poked at the soft squirming bundle until it squeaked, and Mark pulled away.

"You promised if I carried to term and let you have it, you'd set me free."

"Not it, my dear, never it."

"You promised." Her eyes glittered maliciously. "Christians like you always keep their promises. Don't they?"

His heart aching, Mark nodded. "I'll not contest the divorce."

For a moment, the woman's gaze softened. "We did have some good times, didn't we, Mark? But, you see, I'm not ready to settle down to a white picket fence or motherhood."

"Divorce is not God's best...."

Again her voice hardened. "Enough, Mark. Daddy's firm will see to everything. I take it all with me, you know that. There'll be nothing for that." She pointed at the bundle. "And nothing for you."

"I know."

"Good bye then. Sir Jefferey is waiting for me."

Watching her leave, Mark felt the door of his heart thud closed. Then a coo brought his attention to the bundle in his arms, and he smiled. "God will take care of us, Michael. Somehow, we'll make it--with God's help."

For all that, a feeling of guilt squeezed his insides. If only, he had handled things differently. If only. But it was too late.

Cuddling the baby in his arms, Mark numbly left the room.

He never did sign the papers making the divorce official. It didn't seem to matter much to Vanessa. She had no intention of settling down.

He prayed she'd realize how much she needed the Lord and not only accept Jesus, but return to the marriage as well. When an accident took her life, Mark couldn't help but feel if he'd only handled things differently....

CHAPTER ONE

*But he that sinneth against me wrongeth his own
soul: all they that hate me love death.* Proverbs 8:36

Gripping the worn leather cover of the steering
wheel, Megan West tried to convince herself she was just
an ordinary unencumbered young woman heading out of
town for her summer vacation. If only the mirror did not
give lie to her attempt to see herself as the self-confident
writer/counselor of twenty five she was, instead of as the
elfin eighteen year old she looked. Her thoughts spun
back... It all seemed so long ago.

"Meggie, you're beautiful."

*"Thanks Jack," She stared up at the handsome 19-
year-old with all the signs of instant infatuation. "You're
beautiful too."*

*She blushed at his chuckle. "Don't be
embarrassed, Meggie. I like that innocent quality in you."*

Her self-worth grew by leaps and bounds under his
manipulative charm.

She hadn't understood that manipulation, not until
much later. It took a concerted effort, prayer and
determination to rebuild what Jack so casually destroyed.

Maybe self-confident was less than the truth. Her too-wide, blue eyes under lush eyelashes held too much sadness, too much hurt, too many secrets.

Was her sudden overwhelming desire to attend the Salstrand reunion another way to avoid dealing with her pain, another way to run away?

Shaking her head, a smile touched the lips that used to smile so easily. Once, long ago, before she met Jack, before she broke her parent's heart by running away to marry the man of her dreams, she compromised both her values and her relationship to God.

Tears blurred the ribbon of road ahead, and she brushed them away impatiently, thinking, "I've cried enough tears over Jack West. What did it matter anyway? He's dead. Three years dead on foreign soil. My friends think he died a hero."

What a farce! She covered it up then. After his death, Megan took a secretarial course to support herself. Soon afterward, she took courses at a nearby college in counseling and became involved in the local Crisis Pregnancy Center. She could not shake the knowledge that if she had given in to Jack before marriage, the marriage might not have taken place, and she might have found herself with child and no husband.

Abortion would not have been an option for her. More than anything, she wanted to help these girls make the choice for life. How could they know, when trying to decide whether to terminate their pregnancies, how she ached to hold a child, her child, in her arms?

Her pro-life work came to the attention of others, and Megan found herself asked to run a similar agency in Kearney, Nebraska. In Kearney, she was able to leave behind her life with Jack, for in the middle of Nebraska, no one knew the truth about her late husband.

The summer started with dismal rain, which now turned into steaming heat, and her chin-length brunette hair wilted before she hit Grand Island on interstate 80. In the back seats of several passing cars, she glimpsed baseball bats and mitts. They gave mute testimony to how the weather forced the postponement of baseball game after baseball game, far into the sticky hot August days.

The ground had grown soft under the heavy continual moisture. Low pasture land still glistened with pools of water. The corn, too, was late (and short), and she fleetingly wondered how many of the younger students would lose the opportunity to earn money detassling the corn with the season arriving so close to the opening of school.

Even church activities ground to a halt. Though Megan hadn't gotten overly involved, she had found a church home where she didn't feel totally out of place.

The youth pastor's wife befriended her, and, before long, she found herself involved with the youth group. If she could keep even one young person from turning his or her back on faith, the pain of being what she would never be again--carefree--made it worthwhile.

The summer stretched long and dull. At least the dull skies kept her fair skin from burning so easily. Not that it mattered. Since Jack's death, she kept interested men at a distance. As for her friends, they had their own lives, their own work, to keep them busy.

Summer school beckoned. Thumbing through the catalogue, she found not only courses to help her complete a degree in counseling, but also a unique four week course on writing by a visiting professor. Ms. Danver was the consummate world traveler, and she enjoyed the class-- aside from her personal notes about her affairs that stretched from shore to shore. Megan's life seemed dull by comparison, and her small portfolio of published poems an embarrassment beside Ms. Danver's numerous writing credits that included top ranked magazines and newspapers from around the world. She'd also written a book about her travels.

For the most part, Megan passed off the teacher's forays into her lifestyle, just as she did the information on the Salstrand family reunion she received in the mail. On the other hand, Aunt Selma's letter wasn't as easy to ignore. It touched a lonely part of her--a part that longed for family.

After her marriage, she left the fold of her family. Though she tried to sever all ties, her parents didn't let her reluctance stop them from checking in from time to time.

She stuttered, "Mom, Dad. What brings you all the way here?"

Her dad searched her face. "We're here because we're your parents and we love you."

Her mom added, "No matter what, we love you

Megan."

Their love made things more bearable, but her lips remained sealed. By then she hadn't wanted anyone to suspect what she had come to know. Her marriage was not the dream she'd always pictured in her mind, nor Jack the doting husband of her daydreams.

Truthfully, Megan guessed she hid the truth from herself as well. How else could she have passed off the clues so readily available--interrupted phone calls, sudden urges to go out, the late nights? It was almost a relief when he went overseas with his Denver company.

With the death of her parents the year before Jack died, she thought she'd broken all family ties.

Megan thought, *Aunt Selma, bless her heart, never gave up on me.* Though Megan sent pitifully few Christmas cards, she always received one large one with the signature *With Love, Uncle Wally & Aunt Selma.*

Aunt Selma's letter about the reunion arrived before the four week course at the local university began.

Dear Megan,

It has been two years since the last family reunion. We know you were not able to attend, but this year is perfect for you. Since, as you wrote last Christmas, with the hiring of an assistant, you should be able to take some time off. August will be a perfect opportunity to get away.

The reunion runs for a week, starting the first weekend in August. The family has secured the use of a resort in northern Minnesota for our exclusive use. Most of us have had our reservations in for six months or more, but we will be glad to make room for you.

Your uncle Walfred and myself have a cabin all to ourselves, and we would be happy to share the pull-out couch with you. Say you'll come. Love to see you again.

She'd also enclosed several brochures about the area and the resort. They were spread out now on the seat beside Megan, threatening to slide onto the gray carpet of the used luxury car that Jack purchased for himself. An old model, it was a sturdy car and served her well. It was one of the few things she kept from her marriage.

Five Geese Flying Lodge & Resort. The pictures engendered images of cool Northern Pine forests, shimmering lakes, swimming and boat rides. The ideal vacation. The idea glimmered. She should take a vacation. Janice, her assistant, told her she was getting burned out and was probably right. Megan couldn't recall when she had last taken some time off just for herself.

In fact, since the letter came, she toyed with the thought of extending the vacation to a couple of days in Minneapolis first.

Information on the Mall of America also beckoned. A day of shopping. Alone? Well, she'd gotten used to being alone over the last years. Jack hadn't encouraged roots. The secret of their marriage, and his death, made it easier to keep others somewhat at a distance.

Megan grimaced. "I will *not* be hurt nor taken in by a charming manner or a handsome face." She'd had her taste of marriage and had no intention of allowing herself that kind of vulnerability again.

Not that it mattered. Rubbing the cramp in her thigh, she grimaced. Was it the accident that changed Jack or had the signs always been there if she had but taken her parent's advice to stop and consider? She had known almost from the first that he drank. Why hadn't that bothered her more? Why had she been so blind?

Without conscious thought, her finger traced the ridged scar up her leg to her hip. It repulsed Jack. Who could blame him? It repulsed her as well and kept her out of a swimsuit for years. Though it faded over the years and could be erased temporarily with cosmetics, she knew it was still there. And she still tired easily.

Too, she knew there would be no normal relationship for her with a man. Megan's hands clenched the wheel. How could she reveal that scar to anyone's gaze?

Overhead, the grayish clouds folded into themselves like undulating cloud waves. The darkening underpinning echoed her dark thoughts and confused emotions.

Another exit sign seemed to fly by as the car ate up the miles. To the right, bushy deep-green trees crawled up the side of the hill. The rather scraggly Nebraska trees, scattered here and there or clustered about the distant farm houses, portrayed the green foliage of summer.

Home. The word sounded foreign. The reunion? It had been so long. Would anyone else welcome her back? Few had even tried to maintain contact. Would she now be considered an intruder? She had never gone to any of the past reunions and didn't know many of those who had begun to gather every few years so that family ties would not only be maintained, but expanded.

As the interstate turned outside of Lincoln and headed north to Omaha, a screaming green and white semi whizzed by. Her heavy vehicle scarcely moved, but a small import in front of her waffled as though hit by a giant wave.

Import? Why did it always come back to Jack and that last year overseas? Megan thought she had buried the secret with her escape to Nebraska. How was she to know it would come out like it did, in front of a roomful of college students? Her cheeks burned at the memory.

Ms. Danver, Professor Danver, began the day as usual, telling about her six-month stay in Germany. She quickly moved on to her favorite subject, her love life--the theme of her book.

"He was so charming and wonderful. He knew the country and was a satisfying lover, let her tell you." Her gaze held every male eye in class.

"We visited museums and fairs. Drank at local pubs." Her lips turned up in a sly grin. "Tested out the local inns. Let me tell you about the customs we ran into. This is a poem I wrote about it, and here," she held up a slick well-known magazine as she continued, "is the article I wrote about German customs. Remember, gist for your writing must come from life--your experience, your feelings, your emotions."

For a time, her talk turned more general, and

Megan relaxed. The next day, after a pop quiz, the teacher again continued in the same vein. The portrait she drew verbally made Megan inwardly squirm, especially since Professor Danver made perfectly clear her disdain for morality and ethics and Christianity.

In the discussion period, one of the young men, with the audacity of youth, asked, "Since this is the last day of class, how about telling us what happened to this man? Where is this paragon now? You aren't married, so I take it you two didn't make your arrangement legal."

The class sniggered.

"Not my style. I have too much living to do to settle down with one man." Ms. Danver's smile faded, and Megan sensed her pain. Had she really loved this man? Had he ended the relationship, not her? Megan could understand the sense of betrayal she must have felt, though the professor tried hard not to show it.

"He was already married," she snapped, then quietly added, "He's dead. He died soon after I left the country." She smiled then, faintly. "Jack died as he lived, in the arms of a beautiful woman."

Megan's faint gasp drew her attention. "Megan," she said carelessly, "Jack shared your last name."

Megan died a thousand deaths when all eyes turned toward her, though she managed to gulp out, "Common name that."

On the way out of class, one of the girls, with whom she'd gotten acquainted through the church youth group, asked. "Wasn't Jack the name of your husband?"

Her lies tumbled down like a house of cards and, with them, all her defenses. Sucking in her breath, she hastily made her escape from the building. Tears clouded her vision, as she jammed her foot on the gas and jerked away from the curb.

Her humiliation was complete. "Oh, God, how could you let anyone find out about Jack?" Soon everyone at church would know the truth. Megan didn't think she could stand the knowing look in their eyes or the sly questions.

When she returned to her small apartment, she spotted Selma's letter on the counter. Almost before she knew it, she picked up her cell and found herself dialing the number for Five Geese Flying Lodge. "I am part of the Salstrand family. Would you still have room for me?"

"Someone canceled out? A condo. One bedroom. Price. Umm." She could handle that. "Yes, yes please. Reserve it for me, please." Megan fumbled for her wallet. "Here's my credit card number." She read it slowly over the receiver. "Yes, that's it. Thank you."

Setting down the phone, she sucked in a deep breath. She'd have to notify Janice she was leaving in two days. Janice could handle the job in her absence. In fact, sometimes Megan thought Janice ran the center better than she did. No, she wasn't needed in Kearney, not right now at any rate.

Two days later, she headed north.

CHAPTER TWO

Hope deferred maketh the heart sick: but when the desire cometh, it is a tree of life. Proverbs 13:12

Taking a hand from the wheel, Megan adjusted her music choices to bring up Vivaldi. She wasn't so confident a driver that she could take her gaze from the road for more than a moment. Even so the car swerved slightly as she advanced her music.

Vivaldi would have to play until she reached her destination in Omaha, the home of Sam and Dan Matthews. Sam, short for Samantha, had once been a close friend. Megan stood up for Sam when she married the tall, slender Dan Matthews. It seemed so long ago.

Sam's beautiful wedding, the white dress, the flowers, the smiles and the loving family made her want to run away and hide. Already, the novelty had worn off of her own simple wedding. Her hurried justice-of-the-peace ceremony had been so different, without family or dress or flowers or even a minister's blessing. The ceremony had been cold and sterile, and Jack never understood why it all bothered her so much.

"We're hitched. We're legal. What more do you want? Who needs all that fussing?"

Megan merely smiled and hid her tears. She brought it on herself. How could she stand in front of a minister when she knew full well she deliberately chose her husband, contrary to the Biblical principle about marrying a believer? She could hear her father solemnly reciting the verses: *Be not unequally yoked together with unbelievers: for what fellowship hath righteousness with unrighteousness? and what communion hath light with darkness? And what concord hath Christ with Belial? or what part hath he that believeth with an infidel?*[1]

The thought of her hypocrisy still left a sick feeling inside. Mom and Dad tried so hard to raise their daughter to love and serve Christ Jesus.

"Don't worry," she told them. "I've set limits. I know the difference between right and wrong. Don't you trust me to do the right thing?" So adamant, the young.

Megan avoided glancing at the youthful image in the mirror. She didn't feel young, not inside anyway.

A car slowed ahead of her. Pulling into the next lane, she passed him on the multi-lane highway. She never liked cars passing her car in the opposite direction and just a few feet away.

Her hands on the wheel relaxed when the median widened the distance between the lanes of cars and trucks.

---

[1]

II Corinthians 6:14-15 KJV

A bright purple cab rushed in the opposite direction. The driver probably headed home after a long day at work. A single motorcyclist tinkered with his machine. Megan shuddered.

"Lord, please don't let anything go wrong with the car." She had no notion how to take care of the car. Jack had done that and done it well. The air conditioning in the sturdy vehicle hadn't worked for over a year. Without Jack to repair the car, Megan took it in to a garage only to discover it was too expensive to repair. She looked at newer cars, but somehow could not see going into debt when her car, other than the AC, worked perfectly fine.

The air from her half-open window cooled her arm that rested on the door frame. Momentarily, she leaned toward the window, letting the breeze cool her face as well. The breeze, freshening her cheeks and fanning her damp hair, was a nice change from the sticky heat of early afternoon. The air carried the scent of trees, shrubs, damp grass and other growing things, as well as the odor of oil, grease and smoke.

Megan sent up a quick "thanks" for the easing of the heat.

Before she realized it, Megan passed the Omaha city limit sign. Her stomach knotted as she searched the signs for the appropriate turn-offs. Nervously, she clutched the wheel as cars and trucks, many with horns honking, roared down the highway. How did city people deal with this rush all the time?

"Probably find myself on the other side of the city

before I get off the interstate," she muttered through clenched teeth, while she tried to maintain a more manageable speed.

Ahead, to her relief, she saw the sign that confirmed what the GPS told her and moved into the right lane heading into a long curve. "It's a bit tricky," she heard Sam tell her once again as she explained to her friend over the phone. "The road loops around, over and under, and you think you're heading right back to the highway, but you aren't."

Over and under, she followed directions. Stop. Turn. Wait for a red light. Move ahead among commuters going home. The road narrowed. Sounds of the city faded. The stands of trees hovering near the roadway interspersed with fields of bright green. After taking another turn down a quiet street, she drove into an enclave of homes.

The design of the homes proclaimed their upper middle-class status, and she almost felt like an intruder on the quiet street. After checking the address, she pulled into the wide driveway of a one-story house. Painted gray, the house sported darker gray trim set off with artistic touches of mauve and white. The whole presented a subtle elegance.

The house was quiet, too quiet, and no cars stood in the drive. Next door, a balding man tossed a ball to a toddler who was encouraged by a smiling young mother sitting in a wheelchair. At the sight of the little boy in the blue jumpsuit waddling over to present the ball to his mother, the familiar ache began inside. Closing her eyes,

Megan turned from the tender scene.

They could probably tell her when to expect her friends, but she didn't have the nerve to call out to them.

Instead, she combed her hair and touched up her make-up while she waited for either Sam or Dan to return.

"Lord, thank you for getting me here safely," she said aloud. Even before Jack's death she turned to God in her times of need. Afterward, she found her need almost too great and closed herself off. Both the secret of her marriage and the circumstances of Jack's death lay heavy upon her, and her faith continued to suffer. After all, she had been the one to walk away from her faith.

After Jack's death, slowly, step by step, she returned. Step by step, like that toddler next door, she was learning to walk by faith, but it was hard to trust—anyone--again. She had no right to demand anything from the God she spurned for a more physical relationship. True, she managed to hold Jack off until after they signed the wedding papers, but it was a hollow victory. In accepting Jack, she relinquished all that made her who she was inside.

He claimed, *"I won't go to church, Meggie, but I won't stop you."*

But he had. In subtle and not-so-subtle ways, Jack managed to sever her ties with church, and church-related activities. It was easier to give in, than to face his taunts or worse--his anger.

Dan, pulling up beside her in his car, forced her from her gloomy memories. This trip offered much, too much time for morbid introspection. With dismay, she thought about the even longer drive to the Twin Cities the next day.

"Megan, you made it!" Dan's grinning face peered into the window. "Sam should be along any moment."

"Do you want me to move my car?"

He considered a moment. "Leave it. I'll pull into the garage. Sam can leave her car out for now." Dan slid back into his car and pushed a button to open the garage door before proceeding.

Sam drove into the drive as Dan exited the garage. Pulling open her car door, she ran her fingers through her cap of dark hair before reaching to hug Meg. Laughing, Meg, hugged her back. Megan grabbed her purse and followed Sam to the front door that Dan gallantly held open.

With a grin, he patted his wife's bulging middle as she passed. "How's our little Adam doing?"

Sam wrinkled her nose at him. "Sara is doing just fine," she shot back, stepping inside.

As Megan entered, the couple embraced. Their obviously loving relationship grated, and she avoided staring as they murmured softly together.

The entry opened into a vaulted living room, which, while not large, seemed spacious and comfortable.

"Here, let me give you the ten-cent tour," Sam said. "Dan will bring in your luggage and the supplies for supper I bought on the way home."

Megan protested, "No."

Sam's shoulder drooped. "No?"

"Yes, I want the tour, but no, I don't want you to fix supper. I planned on taking you both out to eat."

On his way out, Dan said, "No need."

"I want to."

Sam sighed. "It does sound nice." Megan noticed the lines of exhaustion around the eyes of her friend.

"Sam, you need to sit down. With the baby to think of and all..." She foundered.

"I am fine, just tired. I haven't been working full-time since Monday, so it isn't too bad." She linked her arm with Megan's. "Come on, let me show you around. You have to see the nursery."

The nursery was the last place she wanted to go, but she smiled and allowed Sam to lead her to the room she'd re-decorated. "Dan and I painted and stenciled the walls ourselves," Sam said with obvious pride as she smoothed her delicate hand over the green and white wall.

Four feet off the floor, a border of cowboys and cowgirls riding red, black and gold horses ringed the room. A dark wood crib stood in the corner. The mattress and bumper pad continued the theme of the border as did the musical mobile hanging over the crib. A changing table waited on another wall, and an old fashioned rocker waited in front of wide windows.

Stroking the padded rocker, Sam smiled softly. "Dan's father repaired this old chair for us. His folks are almost as excited about this baby as Dan."

Trying to ignore the sharp pain inside, Megan said,

"Dan does seem pretty excited."

Sam glanced at her. "Of course he is. He'll be a terrific father. It's too bad...." At the expression on Megan's face, Sam hugged her.

"I'm so sorry about Jack," she said. "If he hadn't gotten killed, you'd probably already have a child, maybe two, and you'd be all full of advice."

"I don't know about that." Megan turned away so her friend couldn't see the truth in her eyes.

Jack had been adamant. *"I don't want any brats."*

"What if I get pregnant?" she teased, then drew back at the anger in his eyes.

"Then I'll take you down to the nearest family planning clinic to get it taken care of."

Megan couldn't believe her ears. "Taken care of?"

He shrugged, "You know. An abortion."

"I couldn't. That's murder!"

He sneered. "Let me make this perfectly clear, Meggie. I married you. I wanted you. Just the two of us, understand? If you want me to stay around, don't even think of presenting me with a little 'surprise' some day."

Something died within her that day. Megan made certain that she didn't get pregnant. The one thing she learned quickly enough was that Jack would not be crossed. Absently, her hand touched her cheek. Realizing what she did, she jerked it back, but the look in Sam's eyes gave her pause.

Did her friend suspect all had not been well between them? Years of secrets forced a smile to her lips, along with the appropriate compliments that seemed to divert Sam's attention back to the baby.

"When did you say the little one's due?"

"Another month." Grinning ruefully, Sam rubbed her middle. "Not too soon for me. I feel like a hippo."

Coming into the room, Dan gave her a hug. "Adam will be here before you know it, darling. Then you can get that figure back."

Sam punched him playfully. "Sara, you mean."

Their playful sparing only underscored their deep affection for each other. Dan's gaze seldom left Sam for long, and Sam seemed to bloom under his attention. Their love and regard for each other underscored for Megan the loneliness of her own life, and pointed out how barren her own marriage had been.

If only, she had seen beyond Jack's surface charm. If only, she'd listened when others suggested caution. If only....

Shaking away this introspection, Megan determined to focus her thoughts on Sam and Dan and their life--not her own disaster. For the most part, she succeeded.

Though she planned to take them out, Sam's exhaustion forestalled Megan's good intentions. Instead, she and Dan made Sam rest. While Megan took care of salad and vegetables, Dan grilled steaks. Over dinner, Sam and Megan reminisced about the past. While Dan looked on indulgently, Megan found herself laughing like a schoolgirl with Sam.

Later, Dan left the two, still reminiscing, in the living room while he went downstairs to watch a game. In a moment of silence, Sam smiled softly. "God has been very good to us, Megan. I'm glad I waited for Dan."

Words choked in Megan's throat as tears filled her eyes.

"Oh, Megan," kind-hearted Sam moaned. "I didn't mean to make you cry. Maybe I shouldn't ask, but you seem so unhappy. I thought it was Jack's death, but...." She hesitated. "It's more isn't it? It was Jack?"

I nodded. "Sam, I am so happy for you, really I am." The confession slipped out before she realized. "I wish I had waited."

Though Sam gently tried to get her to open up, Megan refused to say more. "I'll be praying for you, Megan. Somewhere out there, God has the right man for you."

"No!" she said. "I'll never marry again. Never. Never will I allow myself to be that vulnerable again." Of its own volition, her hand went to her face.

"I am fine as I am," she said, aware that a void inside gave lie to her stubborn declaration.

CHAPTER THREE

Commit thy way unto the Lord; trust also in him;
and he shall bring it to pass. Psalm 37:5

The next morning as Megan left Omaha, the sky held a grayish cast. For a short time a train, with cars stacked upon cars, rolled alongside the interstate until trees separated and the tracks diverged from her course.

Ahead, the highway stretched out dull gray, the white side-strip a mesmerizing ribbon. Only the sounds of Mozart kept her awake.

By seven, the sky began to clear with sunlight gilding the serrated clouds. "Lord, please protect me as I travel today. Please keep the car from breaking down or the tires from going flat. And, Lord, forgive me for being so jealous of Sam. I do wish her the best. May her child be healthy and give her and Dan lots of joy."

Megan choked back the ache inside at the thought of the soon-to-be newborn, warm and secure in Sam's arms. Why did she feel so alienated from her friend? Deliberately, she let her mind wander.

Like her mind, fog drifted over the countryside in a

drizzled haze, fading slowly as the clouds cleared. The sun glinted in her eyes and made her squint. Keeping her eyes on the road, she rummaged in her purse for her sunglasses, which she found and put on.

On either side of the wide highway, that stretched to the horizon, farm houses interrupted the rich green of the hills, the deep emerald of the soy bean fields and the rows and rows of under-ripe corn.

Was there, she wondered, a way out of her own fog as well? Even as the thought surfaced, a deeper fog descended, enveloping her gray car. Smelling of dust and rain, it lifted on the top grades, but continued to hover in the lower places and across the bridges.

Driving through the fog depressed Meg. Tension stiffened the muscles in her shoulders. The album ended abruptly. A glance at the dash showed the gas tank nearly empty. Thankful for an excuse for a break, she pulled off the interstate.

Once off the highway, Megan began to relax. By the time she reached a filling station, eight miles away in a small town boasting an authentic Danish windmill, a smile touched her lips. The coffee shop attached to the filling station must have been the gathering place for all the local businessmen and farmers in the area.

As she opened the glass door to go inside to pay and use the facilities, she cringed at the fifteen pairs of eyes trained on her jean-clad figure. Nervously, she tugged at her "Life is Precious" T-shirt as she plastered a faint smile on her lips. Though she sensed neither harm nor

malice in those gathered, the curious stares made her feel
even more alienated than she did already.

By the time she returned to interstate 80, the sun
had disappeared altogether. The disembodied fog
compounded her feeling of alienation. Phrases tickled her
mind and a poem formed. Out loud she worked and
reworked the lines.

> *He speaks to me through the cold damp mist,*
> *But will I hear his voice?*
> *Does Christ truly care I've lost my way,*
> *Or is the fog my choice?*
>
> *Oh, come to me Lord Jesus,*
> *May I see again your face.*
> *I need the acceptance of your love,*
> *Need again to feel your embrace.*

The words choked in her throat. As usual, her
poems spoke of things she never talked about with anyone.
She thought of the poems already published, poems born
out her anguish over her husband's betrayal and
scandalous death.

This latest work played through her mind along
with the other poems. With surprise, she noted that a
thread of faith, though faint, stood out in each.

"Oh, Lord, is there hope for me?"

A couple of verses sounded so loudly in her mind
she glanced around to see who spoke, but she rode

alone...or did she? Megan mouthed Matthew 11:28-30 that she'd learned in a Sunday School class during her fourth grade year in order to earn some little prize she'd forgotten about now.

Come unto me, all you that labour and are heavy laden, and I will give you rest. Take my yoke upon you, and learn of me; for I am meek and lowly in heart: and you shall find rest unto your souls. For my yoke is easy, and my burden is light.

Rest. He promised rest. How she wanted to rest, to lay down her burden. Why was it so hard? "Help me, Lord," she whispered. "I don't know how. Somehow, I've lost my way."

In the fog that isolated her from the other shadowy vehicles sliding silently through the haze, she sensed timelessness. Megan could have been a thousand years in the future or a century in the past when wagon trains headed west.

She could almost hear the crack of the whip over the plodding oxen, but she headed the wrong direction for the wagons going west to Oregon. Maybe, she was headed the wrong direction.

Near the Mento exit, she exchanged Mozart for Bach. The swelling strains soothed her trouble soul. Like a guiding light, the sun peeped in and out of the clouds. The glimpses of the sun quickened her spirit as well.

By 8:45 a.m., the rays from the sun kissed the feathery clouds forming over the duller gray of early morning. The sun warmed her face, and she felt as though

God himself smiled on her in her gray "slightly battered" car. The large car held up much longer and proved more faithful than the spouse who purchased it with such pride.

Above her head, the unsightly ceiling drew a quick gaze. When the off-white material sagged, she'd pulled it off. The white vinyl seats had numerous tears and the door handle stuck on the passenger side. However, the blue dash board, though dusty, appeared almost new--or would with a good polishing.

Megan kept the front windows open to let the breeze cool her face. She didn't mind the air ruffling her hair, as it did now, for it kept her alert.

Fondly, she patted the dash. The car took her where she needed to go. What more did she want? "We are a lot alike, this car and I."

The miles slid by more quickly than she could have imagined. Closer to Des Moines, she pulled over. She'd studied two routes through the city and growled at the indecision causing her to forget to make a choice for the GPS. With a prayer and a guess, she chose the route suggested by a trucker friend who often travelled the highway.

Biting her lip she whispered, "Lord, I hate city driving. Help me not to mess this up and get lost." She only trusted the GPS so far. Hers had been known to make some whacky choices. Probably needed replacing.

Megan couldn't help but recall a recent news story of a car, full of people, getting lost and turning down a street guarded by a trigger-happy gang. The driver drove out as fast as possible, but not until set-upon by the gang. One of the passengers was shot and killed. With her luck with GPS and sense of direction, she could see something similar happening to her.

Verses from Proverbs three filled her heart. *Trust in the LORD with all thine heart; and lean not unto thine own understanding. In all thy ways acknowledge him, and he shall direct thy paths.*

"Help me trust you, Lord," she prayed as she negotiated the older highway through town. "Help me not to be afraid."

Traffic was amazingly sparse. "Thank you, God, for leading me to this route." When she headed north, and was on the road toward Minneapolis and the treat she promised herself, she finally relaxed.

A full day at the mall sounded pretty good.

As the sky cleared and the sun shone down warm and bright, she hummed quietly along with the music. At Dowd, Iowa she pulled off the highway to take a much needed break and stopped in front of the welcome center, a converted train depot. The small, dark-wood log station held knick-knacks and souvenirs in glass counters around a pot belly stove. Wooden benches welcomed the weary, while racks displayed brochures about Iowa. Megan used the modern bathroom before picking up a couple of brochures.

A thin, elderly man motioned toward an open book. "Would you please sign our register? It lets the state commission know how many people come through here."

With a smile, she complied before leaving. Back in the car, she chose the older album "This is the Life" which the youth pastor's wife told her to listen to on the drive.

"I think you'll like this," she said. "He's a Christian comedian. It's old, one of his first, but I felt you could use this."

Megan tried to show some enthusiasm. "Sounds great."

Back on the interstate, she expected an hour of laughter, but there was much more to the music than jokes.

Enclosed alone in the large car with the album playing in the background, Megan felt disconnected from the world around her. The words drew her attention. The comedian talked about times of trusting God, about his car accident, about his injuries.

Numb, she listened as her own hurts and pain surfaced. Shaking her head, she fought the memories. No, she didn't want to face those memories. Had she not buried them forever? She didn't want to face the depth of Jack's deception and depravity. She didn't want to face her own responsibility in choosing a man she never should have married; a faith she never should have abandoned.

Over and over, she blinked back tears, trying to focus on her driving, passing slower cars and staying in the right lane. Her stomach growled, bringing her back to more mundane things. With a laugh, she pulled off in Clear Lake and looked for a fast-food burger place. Megan followed a two-toned blue and silver mini-van into the parking lot.

Locking the doors, she glanced over at the tussled-haired youngster, she guessed to be about seven or eight, eagerly hopping out of the mini-van. His foot caught on a crack in the pavement. With a gasp, he fell in front of a car zooming through the parking lot. Instinctively, she snatched him out of the way and brushed off his jeans.

"Thanks Lady."

His wide blue eyes caught hers, and a grin spread across his mischievous face. Megan couldn't help but grin back. For a heartbeat, she thought she witnessed a certain sadness in the depths of those wide eyes. As he dashed around the vehicle to his father, she stifled her envy at his eagerness and hoped his parents appreciated the engaging lad. How different this trip would be if she had a child with whom to share the experience.

Shrugging the thought aside with some difficulty, she entered the establishment and ordered a small hamburger with the works, fries and a small drink. The small burger joint was almost full, but she found a table for one and sat down. Curious about the boy's folks, she glanced around to locate the lad. She caught a glimpse of wide shoulders and heard the boy's chatter. From her vantage point, she couldn't see the boy's mom. Did he have one?

The man's deep tones held a trace of sadness that touched a cord deep inside. Maybe what she witnessed in the lad's gaze hadn't been her imagination. Something about the stranger drew her.

She found herself straining to hear his voice, heard

a hint of humor and listened to the boy's delighted giggle. The man's deep times sent a shiver of excitement down her spine. What was it with her anyway? She didn't even know the guy and he affected her.

With a frown, Megan threw away the packaging from her lunch before exiting into the warm sunshine. The clouds floated in fluffy puffs across the sky. "Lord, am I really that needy?"

Heat emanated from the car when she pulled on the burning silver handle and slipped onto the steaming vinyl seat. Starting the car, she lowered the windows before finding her way back to the interstate.

She listened as the comedian/singer crooned, "Go with God. Go with God, and He will go with you."

Somehow, the message touched and released something deep within. "Go with God."

Come unto me, all you that labour and are heavy laden, and I will give you rest.

"I will give you rest."

As the album ended, tears began to flow. For the first time, she saw her arrogance in trying to go her own way even while praying for God's will. From the first, she allowed him only the most minute part of her life.

Hardest to admit was that Jack was not the problem. She was. She had never truly given Christ first place in her life. She thought she could be a Christian on her own terms, but she failed. Oh, how she'd failed. When Jack came along, she fell not because of Jack, but because of her own rebellious heart.

When Jack died, she'd shoved it all into the back recesses of her mind. His shameful secret was a reflection on her, and on the person she wanted others to see. *Oh, God, forgive me.*

In the next two hours, God and Megan got a lot of things straightened out. By the time she reached the Hope exit, she was humming, "Go with God. Go with God." How appropriate. She smiled.

The sun seemed brighter and the sky a deeper blue. Inside, for the first time in years, she knew hope and forgiveness and a new start.

There was much yet with which she needed to deal and more pain to walk through. But she knew God was real. God did care. And, deep within, a healing had begun.

Smiling through tears, she cried out as she raised a hand. "Thank you, Lord. Thank you, Lord. Thank you." Maybe she needed this vacation more than she realized.

CHAPTER FOUR

*He shall give his angels charge over thee, to keep
thee in all thy ways. They shall bear thee up in their
hands, lest thou dash thy foot against a stone.*
                                    Psalm 91:12-13

The anticipation she felt as she approached
Minneapolis did not quite cover the clutch of her middle
and the sweat on her palms as more and more vehicles, all
traveling faster than the speed limit, whizzed by.

Was a trip to "the large, fully enclosed retail and
family complex," (Megan recalled the phrase from a
brochure), worth this assault of fear? She loved to shop,
even it meant only window shopping. While multiple
floors and hundreds of specialty stores seemed
intimidating, it also made her mind simmer with the
possibilities.

How much more interesting the trip would be with
a companion. She sighed as the scene of the man and his
son flashed in her mind. She heard again his deep, caring
voice; the boy's laugh and shivered. She had to get that
image from her mind. The two did not belong to her, did

not belong in her heart or on her mind. Jack had insulated her from marriage, she told herself firmly as the anticipation of a day without responsibility surfaced.

The reality of entering the city itself overlay the excitement with the terror of driving alone in the metropolis where cars and trucks and motorcycles shot by, heedless of the congested traffic. Exits and signs and on ramps all passed in a jumble, and she tensed. Her leg ached from the long drive, and she grimaced, wishing she'd taken something for the pain earlier. Too late now.

Once more, the sun disappeared behind a bank of clouds. The trees, more and more of them evergreens, grew taller here. More and more patches of woodland hemmed in the road.

Huge signs flashed overhead before she could read them, and a thousand routes led off left and right. She tried to follow the GPS voice. Nervously, she checked left and right, trying to stay in the lane that would take her to the motel complex across from the mall where she had made a reservation.

Would she see her turn-offs in time? Would she be able to change lanes when needed?

Gulping back her fear, she turned off onto one highway, then another, and another until she headed north on a two-lane street leading straight toward her destination. To her relief, traffic thinned, and she had little trouble finding the towering inn. Pulling up into the parking lot, she flicked off the ignition. Sighing, Megan leaned back, letting the tension leave her body.

Gathering the remnants of her strength, she picked up her purse and a small overnight bag, before heading toward the fluted glass entryway. The dark, brick-face opened to a vaulted interior of blonde-wood. Check-in was painless, thanks to her reservation, and she was shown to a room down a long hall and around the corner from the main desk.

The quiet elegance of the English decor further settled her, as did her room which was decorated in restful shades of green and lilac and baize. The quilt on the bed carried out the color scheme, as did the forest-green, painted, iron bed frame.

Exhausted, she put down her bag and purse on the small table next to the television entertainment center and flopped down on the bed. She melted into the solid but comfortable mattress. A moment later, her eyes closed.

When she awoke, powerful spot lights bouncing light off the dark sky streamed through her open shades. Yawning, she slowly got up to snap on the lamp before closing the shades. From the menu she found on the table, she checked the food selection of the restaurant attached to the inn and placed an order.

Soup and salad settled nicely. Setting the cart outside the door, she pulled off her clothes and threw them into her bag. After a bath, Megan settled on the bed. Restlessly, she picked up the remote control and flicked through the channels, but nothing caught her interest.

Her mind wondered to the little boy at the burger place, who had grinned at her so unself-consciously.

Something about him pulled at her heart, but she steeled against such impossible sentiment. Why waste time mooning about a young lad she'd never again see.

Again, she felt the deep ache inside, but this time she allowed the truth to penetrate.

"Lord," she said, "I can't hide the truth any longer. I want a child of my own. My arms ache to hold, to hug. Yet, I am not ready for a relationship." Megan laughed softly. "Lord, I don't even know anyone I'd like to date, much less marry."

Like a child she asked, "Is marriage possible for me again? Is there someone for me, or have I destroyed my chances through my deliberate disobedience?"

No answer sounded in the quiet of the room, but her gaze fell on the Gideon Bible laying on the nightstand.

Picking it up, she idly thumbed through it. The pages fell open to Psalms 37. Verse four leaped out at her as though underlined. *Delight thyself also in the Lord; and he shall give thee the desires of thine heart.*

If only she had done that before she met Jack, how different her life might have been. Though she couldn't change the past, she could look ahead. Was it possible that Jesus loved her enough to give her, her heart's desire? Was there a man, a child, in her future?

Delight thyself also in the Lord. Delight; be joyful; be glad. Did that mean serving God was not the tedious, mechanical function she once believed? Megan thought of her healing communication with God on the way to the city.

"Oh, Lord, help me to serve you with joy. Thank you for your healing and forgiveness." Somehow she couldn't hope for more.

With that on her mind, she finished drying her hair, crawled under the covers and fell into the most peaceful sleep she'd known for years.

She awoke to a day gray with rain. Yet it did little to dampen the excitement that gripped her. After pulling on a pair of black jeans and a soft rose cotton shirt with long sleeves to ward off the cooler weather, she stuffed her wallet and other essentials into a small black canvas cross-body purse and anchored it around her neck. She was not going to become the victim of a theft if she could prevent it. Besides, she wanted her hands free to look and touch.

The tour book said the inn provided their guests with a continental breakfast. Glancing around the lobby at families out for a day's adventure, she spotted a couple anxious to be on their way, and businessmen, mainly Asian, in crisp business suits waiting rather sternly with their heavy luggage. Others moved toward a room, decorated in dark green, beyond the lobby. Guests quickly filled the chairs around the small square tables. Chatter, as well as intermittent laughter, also filled the room.

Getting into line, she found far more than the simple rolls and coffee. Megan could choose between several different kinds of cereals, rolls, donuts and fruit, along with milk and juice or coffee. Picking up a bowl, she chose whole wheat cereal, added milk, juice and a banana. Finding a table in the corner, she sat down to eat.

High on the far wall, a light from a TV screen flickered over the room. Glancing at the screen, she tried to hear the topic on the talk show, but turned away in disgust at its sexual content. Surveying the room, she found that, like her, most ignored the program.

Suddenly, all the guests looked upward as the news announcer broke in with news of a severe storm. Residents of some locales were asked to take cover, but she couldn't hear at what locations.

Outside, rain splashed the sidewalk and ran down the long picture windows, but business continued as usual as guests came and went in their own vehicles or in the transportation provided to the airport. Megan didn't have long to wait for the first bus to the Mall. Though she contemplated walking, the rain changed her mind. Besides, the weather also made her leg ache, and she sent up a prayer.

"Lord, please help me get around today, and don't let my leg hurt too much." Megan put action to words by popping down a couple of mild pain killers.

The Inn shuttle bus driver was an older man with a ready smile. He joked with the passengers as he drove to, actually under, the Mall. The set down point was deep under the complex. With its eerie echoing sounds and deep shadows, it seemed like the perfect setting for a murder mystery.

The driver let the riders off with the admonition, "I pick up right here every hour. Last bus at 8 p.m. Miss it and you walk back."

Megan thought it would be easy to find her way up, but it took several tries before she found an elevator. She could use stairs, but they had a way of exhausting her quickly, and she wanted to save her strength for shopping!

Finally, she found her way up onto the 2nd floor of a giant anchor department store. After a quick look around, she moved on. She could look at their merchandise any time. The walk-way hugged the sides, then yawned open from top to bottom. Dizzy from looking down, Megan hastily backed away from the rail.

More or less to take a quick inventory, she popped in and out of several stores as she made her way toward the center of the Mall, where the roar of motors and the excited shouts and laughter of children drew her.

Already weary, she used the ramp down to the eating tables. Megan perched on the table and leaned over the wooden fence railing to take in the amusement park totally enclosed within the mall. A cacophony of colorful sights and noisy, happy sounds slammed into her ears.

From her vantage point, she picked out a roller coaster or two, adventure rides, the usual carousel and all sorts of kid's rides. Screams rose with the height and speed of the rides, echoing and re-echoing throughout the immense gray structure. Below her, a myriad of people of different races good-naturedly jockeyed for position in front of the many side shows and games shoe-horned into the tight floor space.

How fun it would be to ride some of the rides.

There wasn't much excitement in being alone at a fair--no strong arm to clutch, no companion with whom to share the joys and the fright and no child to scream in laughter.

She shook her head, refusing to feel sorry for herself. Megan promised herself a day of relaxation and shopping, not one of mooning over what she did not possess--a child. She tasted the bitterness at the denial of that joy. She tried to banish thoughts of the man and his son as they edged into her thoughts.

"Oh, Lord, will I ever truly heal? Will I ever be worthy to be a wife and mother?"

Glancing over the waist-high barrier, she watched a young boy clutching a stuffed bear, his shining eyes gazing rapturously up at the tall, broad shouldered man at his side, a man whose face she could not see. With a start, she recognized the boy from the fast-food place in Clear Lake.

At the same moment, he glanced up and waved a hand while flashing his engaging smile. With a grin, she started to wave back, then dropped her hand as the man's head shot up and a frown deepened the lines that knifed from his nose to his mouth.

Megan gulped at the dark eyes, relieved when they glanced down at the boy who tugged at the belt of his casual slacks. Without hearing a word of the conversation, she read the boy's explanation in his animated face and expressive hands. Her heart pounded. "Lord, what are you doing?"

Leaning back, she got off the table, intending to

leave the amusement park that brought back not only pleasant childhood memories of country fairs, but a deep sadness as well. Automatically, her hand felt for her purse as she started toward the exit. She couldn't face the man whose profile and voice refused to leave her thoughts—at least not for long.

An small voice called, "Please wait up."

Thinking some child spoke to his parent, she continued on until a small hand grabbed her arm. Swinging around, she met the pleading face of the little boy.

"Please, we want to talk to you." His hurt, wide-eyed gaze cut her heart.

Megan smiled down at him. "I'm sorry. I didn't realize you were calling to me."

"Oh." The smile returned. "That's all right then."

Questioningly, she glanced into the slightly red-tinged face, a handsome face she noted absently, of his father. "May I help you?"

"Yes, yes," the boy cried. "I want you to ride with us."

"Me, but...."

"Son, I told you, the lady probably has other plans."

Suspicion filled her mind. Was the man using the boy to pick her up while his wife shopped? Surreptitiously, she looked at his ring finger. Only a faded strip around his finger proclaimed his once-married status. Oh, not!

Divorced? Had he dumped his poor wife? She thought of Jack. After hearing in glowing detail of his affair with her professor, she didn't doubt that, sooner or later, Jack would have walked out on their so-called marriage as well. Anger burned within her against men like Jack and like this tall stranger whose face held a certain hesitation.

When she didn't speak, he said, "Michael told me what you did for him yesterday at that stop in Iowa, and I wanted to thank you. He could have been seriously injured." His pain was real enough, and she softened toward the man.

He set a large hand on the lad's shoulder. "I wish he would have told me then so we could have thanked you immediately."

Michael blinked shyly. "Daddy, you always told me not to run without lookin', and I didn't want you mad at me."

Again suspicion lurked. Did this huge man abuse the child? He must have read some of that in her hesitation, and a mask dropped over his face. "Come Michael, the lady is too busy to join us."

"Join you?" she echoed in surprise.

"Yes." Michael grinned. "I asked Daddy if we could ask you to come on the rides with us."

"I...I. What about your mother?"

The father's eyes sparked, and it was the little boy who answered. "We don't talk about her, Miss. She's gone."

Megan's heart ached for what that woman was missing. "Oh." She didn't know what to say. Was the man trying to pick her up? Who was he anyway?

With a sigh, the boy's father stuck out his hand. "May we start again? Hello. My name is Mark Adrian, father of this scamp here." He ruffled the boy's shaggily cut hair as Michael grinned at him.

"I am a respectable businessman from Salina, Kansas on vacation with his son. No, I am not married. And, if I was, I wouldn't be trying to pick up some stranger." His face twisted into a half frown, half smile. "Or a friend either. It's just that, that Michael has taken to you, and he asked. No strings."

"You will come with us, won't you?" Michael tugged at her arm, and she found it nearly impossible to ignore the plea in his eyes.

Absently, she rubbed her leg. "Well, it does sound like fun." *If my leg doesn't give out*, she thought. What did it matter? One day of fun, isn't that what she promised herself?

Taking Mark's hand, she said, "Mark Adrian, my name is Megan West from Kearney, Nebraska." The touch of his hand sent unexpected warmth to her cheeks.

He continued to hold her hand. "And what do you do in Kearney, Nebraska, Miss--it is Miss--," at her nod, he continued, "West?"

"I supervise a Crisis Pregnancy Center. We want the girls' to know there is an alternative to abortion."

Respect flashed in Mark's eyes. "We need many

more like you Miss West." The look he bestowed on his son stopped her heart. "Too many babies d.." Mark glanced toward his wide-eyed son. "Are lost without caring and direct intervention."

Megan knew he almost said die. Had Michael's life, this precious treasure, ever been in doubt?

Gulping back the questions flooding her mind, Megan chose one of the more innocuous ones. "What do you do in Kansas?"

"Run the family business," he watched her closely as he added, "A Christian bookstore."

"Really!" She smiled in relief. "Are you a Christian then?"

No hesitation this time. "Absolutely. And you?"

For some reason, tears started in her eyes. Megan blinked them away with a half laugh. "Oh, yes. Yes." The two grinned at one another.

Michael asked in exasperation, "Well, you gonna come with us?"

"Yes, I will. How do I go about getting tickets?"

"No." Mark brushed this away. "My treat."

Michael grabbed first her hand, then his Dad's. "Come on then. I want to ride the roller coaster and the train and the...."

Laughing, Megan let herself be pulled along. Up, up, up, they inched on the roller coaster and zoomed down. Air rushed into her face, and she laughed along with Michael, feeling almost as young and free as he. Mark indulged them both.

When she stumbled on the stairs, he not only steadied her, but wrapped a protective arm around her waist. Megan went on every ride possible, then she joined Mark to watch Michael on the children's rides. Giggling, he waved at them. Mark won prizes for them all at the shooting gallery, and Megan gave her giant inflated hand to Michael.

The three collected so much stuff, Mark halted. "I cannot carry another thing. How about we get a locker for this stuff."

After Mark locked the locker and put the key in his pocket, Michael said, "I'm hungry."

Mark nodded toward Meg. "Where do you want to eat?" His question made her stop.

The morning had been a pleasant diversion, but she didn't plan on hanging onto this father-son duo. There was no doubt the two adored each other, and if sometimes she caught a sadness in the eyes of the father, she put it out of mind. She had enough problems of her own without taking on any more.

Fleetingly, she wondered about the boy's mother. Was she dead? Did that explain that sadness in Mark's eyes, and the hunger in the boy for a woman's touch?

"I thank you for a lovely time," she stuttered, "but I suppose I really should be going. I promised myself a day of shopping."

Mark raised an eyebrow. "Before you eat?"

Michael all but begged. "Eat with us. Eat with us. Pl...ease."

"I don't wish to further impose on you."

"So that's it." Mark took her arm. "No argument now. Let's find someplace to eat."

Michael decided on the fast-food shops in the amusement area. To her embarrassment, Megan ordered a small shake, then immediately dropped it. Mark scooped it up, and, with a minimum of fuss, replaced it before shepherding them to a small round table.

They made small talk. Megan relaxed in easy companionship. "You come up here often?"

Michael shook his head as his dad answered. "No, we're headed north for a vacation."

Megan smiled. "Me, too. Family reunion."

After dinner, Megan insisted she leave, but somehow shopping wasn't all that much fun alone, though she did purchase a royal blue cap with the word SWEDEN stamped across the front, several T-shirts with the mall logo, some souvenir postcards and several magazines.

Exhausted, she hobbled to the elevator, and made her way down to the underground parking lot to catch the last shuttle bus. There she found Mark and Michael waiting as well. Michael welcomed her with a big smile.

"Hi, Miss West," he called.

"Hi, Mike."

"Michael," he corrected.

Mark followed his son to where she waited. "Have a good day?"

"Yes, thank you," she told him. "I see you got all your loot down here."

Mark made a face at the assortment of trinkets and balloons and packages. "Probably won't let us on the bus."

"Where are you staying?"

"One of the Holiday Inn's. You."

"The inn across the street."

The conversation lagged as they watched bus after bus arrive from different motels, pick up their guests and leave.

"I'm sorry about the boy's mother," Megan said for something to say. "You must miss her dreadfully."

Mark's face hardened. "Don't be," he growled. "And don't worry about Michael. He never knew his mother. She is dead; so forget it."

At that moment, their shuttled bus arrived, and she watched in stunned surprise as he grabbed up their things and herded his son into its interior.

As the shuttle bus pulled away, Michael waved through the window.

Whatever made her ask such a personal question? Kicking herself, she boarded the shuttle bus from Country Inns that pulled up and opened its doors.

She felt she had lost a friend.

CHAPTER FIVE

Trust in the Lord, and do good... Psalm 37:3a

Back at the Inn, she entered the lobby juggling her packages. Her leg dragged as she walked, more accurately, limped down the hall and inserted her key card. With a sigh, she dropped the packages on the bed and sat down.

The mall had been less than she expected, and so much more.

"Lord, forgive me for being so nosy. And, and thank you for giving me special memories." The prayer formed on lips almost of its own volition and a sense of joy leaped inside as she realized that she really was in communication with God and that He was listening.

Since it was already late, she contemplated having supper sent in as she had the night before, but decided against it. After freshening up, she pulled out a new T-shirt and pulled it on. It pulled on the shoulders and restricted her movements.

Groaning, she pulled it off to check the tag. Grabbing the other two shirts, she checked them as well. Why hadn't she checked the tags before she purchased them? Silly question. She'd been thinking of Michael and his father and feeling the security of his arm about her waist.

She blushed at the thought as she buttoned on the shirt she'd worn all day. After locking the door, she followed the signs to the connecting restaurant. The smell of steak and fries wafted toward her in the tight quarters of the place with its high-back booths.

"Seating for one?" The thin waitress, somewhere in her late twenties, Megan guessed, snapped out the phrase sounding slightly irritated and bored. The young woman's shoulders slumped with exhaustion, and her face held the hint of a frown.

"Yes," Megan said automatically and was glad when the waitress found her a corner table.

Megan ordered, and soon had, a plate heaping with steak and fries set in front of her.

"Thank you." She smiled at the waitress and received a slight smile in return.

"You're welcome." Did Megan imagine the waitress walked away a little straighter?

Megan enjoyed the food, even as her thoughts turned toward Mark and his needy son. In fact, she found her thoughts invariably led back to them. Shaking her head at herself, she paid her bill and headed back to her room.

After a quick shower, she pulled on her night gown. For sometime she read from the Bible, before turning out the lights and going to sleep.

Awaking late, she pulled on her jeans and a black

T-shirt with a cuddly bear emblazoned across the front. She took advantage of the breakfast provided, then grabbed her purse, made sure she had her receipt for the newly purchased T-shirts, picked up the bag with them inside and left her room. Since she had no intention of shopping, and since the weather had cleared up, she walked to the Mall where she exchanged her small sized shirts for mediums.

Of course once there, she couldn't resist looking around a bit before heading back to the Inn to check out. Around noon, she settled into her car. Unfolding the map, she visually checked the sequence of highways she needed to get on and off. It acted as a check on her GPS—just in case.

After a moment, she bowed her head. "Lord, please protect me while I travel today. Help me get on all the right roads and not get lost." She added for emphasis, "Especially help me with the 'not get lost' part."

Taking 494 to 94 to 101 to 169, she prayed constantly. Both the map and her GPS seemed in perfect harmony, causing her to relax a bit. The traffic Saturday morning was not overly heavy, but keeping track of the road changes made her a nervous wreck. Thankfully, she got onto 169 with only minor difficulties.

The day was perfect for traveling. A few friendly clouds puffed against an azure sky lit with soft sunlight. Her heart light, Megan sang along with praise music as she drove.

Tall, stately trees grew more thickly together as she

traveled north and were more and more interspersed with cool blue and green lakes. Pine faintly scented the clear air.

By the time she reached Milace, the sun disappeared behind a bank of clouds. The air cooled considerably, and Megan raised the window to permit only a hint of breeze. Traffic thinned.

Low land and scrub became green-washed marshes. On a smaller highway, she kept passing signs warning motorists to slow down. She checked her speed. Since the road was smooth and wide, it was easy to forget.

"Lord, I'm glad I'm going to the Salstrand reunion." To her surprise, Megan found herself conversing naturally as she drove and didn't feel nearly so alone as when traveling from Kearney to Minneapolis. A smile touched her lips.

Following a quick check on the GPS, she cut off on 18 toward Brainerd to stock up on groceries, get gas and eat. Though she wasn't overly tired, she knew she needed a break. Once in town, she turned onto 210--the highway that would connect her back to 6 north. Megan was at the edge of town before she realized it. A moment later, she pulled in at a golden arches and sat down to a burger and fries and vanilla shake.

As she ate, she reread all the brochures. "Jay and Rose Mays invite you to be their guest at Five Geese Flying Lodge and Resort. Overlooking Thunder Lake, all cabins are complete with stove, refrigerator, cooking utensils and full bath or shower." Another warned, "Bring your own towels and wash cloths."

When she called for reservations, Rose confirmed that she needed to stock her own personal toiletries and food. Umm. Megan took out a pad of paper and a pen to make a list of groceries and supplies she needed. Back on the road, Megan hunted for a grocery store, stopping at a self-serve country market to stock up on food, toilet paper and other supplies. She also stopped for gas.

Once more on the road, she headed north. Tall, stately red and white pine stood like sentinels on either side of the road. Their Christmasy scent hung heavy in the moisture laden air. She connected up with 6 with little trouble, but the car seemed to be listing to the left.

Concentrating, she compensated, but still it pulled. Licking her lips, she breathed, "Lord, please don't let me be stranded out here. Please let everything be all right, at least until I get to the lodge."

Few towns broke the tight cover of evergreen trees, though white-barked birch showed more and more among the stately red pine. Passing the small town of Outing, she almost stopped, but decided against it. Had she made the right decision?

Fear churned her insides, and her prayers grew more desperate, as the heavy car listed further to one side. It became harder and harder to keep a grip on the steering wheel and the tires on the road. The smell of skunk pervaded the air, and she choked as she gunned the motor, grabbing the wheel as the car jerked toward a car in the opposite lane.

Suddenly she heard a soft pop, and the car dragged the wheel from her hands. Screaming out to God, she wrenched it back and slowly guided it onto the shoulder. Shutting off the car, she leaned back. Her whole body shook as a semi whizzed by on the road.

"Lord, I could have been killed." Megan wiped sweat from her forehead. "Thank you, Lord. Thank you."

After a few moments, Megan collected herself enough to climb out and inspect the damage. A branch had scraped the side, leaving a wide swath. Worse than that, the left front tire had flattened under the heavy vehicle.

Was there a jack in the trunk? And a spare? Megan didn't even know if she had one, much less how to change the tire.

"Lord, it's you and me. How about a quick one-two-three on tire changing?"

Opening the trunk, she gingerly poked through her baggage to find a tire, she hoped it was all right, and a jack. Dragging them out, she lay them down, staring at the tire still on the car. How was she to get it off?

Forgetting the dirt on her hands, she wiped her face. Looking up, she choked, "Now what, Lord?" Megan kicked the tire. "Why couldn't you answer my prayer to keep the car going until I reached the lodge?"

No answer forthcoming, she tried to envision how her father had changed car tires when they went flat. A wrench. He used a wrench. Going back to the trunk, she tried to find what she needed, but found nothing.

What was she going to do? It was a long way back

to the nearest habitation, and who knew what lay ahead. Absently, she rubbed her leg. Megan doubted it would carry her that far. Gulping back her fear, she reached into the car for her purse. As she was locking the car, a silver sports car zipping passed, slowed and backed up. A male voice slurred. "Need help, pretty lady?"

Swinging around, she stared at the naked lust in the man's gaze. He smiled at the fear he witnessed in her own. "I...I'll be okay," she stammered, but he stopped his car, opened the door and stood on rather wobbly, but long legs. His blond hair fell over his pale blue eyes.

"It's my tire," she told him, hoping to keep his mind off of her. "I don't seem to have a wrench."

"I can fix it," he said, then surveyed her so thoroughly she blushed. "What's a nice girl like you doing in a place like this?"

Megan had no intention of telling him any more than absolutely necessary. "Please. Can you fix my tire? I can pay you."

Stepping closer, he tried to draw her into his embrace. "Sure, and I know just what payment I want."

"No!" Megan struggled to get away, but he was too strong. His breath smelled of liquor. Panic licked her mind.

"Jack. Jack let me go. You're drunk."

"And you're mine, for better or worse."

Megan pushed him away. "And this is for the worst," she retorted. "Now, go sleep it off."

His hand gripped her wrist so hard, she cried out.

"I get what she want," he threatened.

So like Jack. "Help me Jesus!" she cried aloud. "Help me."

"Let her go," a familiar voice commanded. She hadn't seen Mark's vehicle pull up.

"I was here first. The lady's mine."

Strong fingers clamped onto the man's shoulder. "I said, let her go." He looked at her. "Are you all right, Megan?"

Rubbing his shoulder, the man glanced from Mark's glowering face to her. "Didn't know the babe belonged to someone else. Need to keep better tab on what's yours." With a scowl toward Mark, the man climbed back in his car, gunned the motor and shot down the road.

"Oh, Mark," Megan hugged herself to keep from shaking. "I'm so glad you came along."

"Me too." Touching her cheek, he grinned. "Nice touch. Early mechanic, I think."

"Oh." Megan tried to rub the grease from her face, but only succeeded in smearing it. Taking out his handkerchief, Mark wiped her face.

"That's better." He hesitated. Whatever he was about to say was drowned out in Michael's eager greeting.

Launching himself at Meg, the boy hugged her. "Are you all right?"

Mark caught her before she fell. Megan liked the feel of his arms, but she pushed away. It would be all-too-easy to let herself fall prey to her own deep needs. This man was much-too-much for her peace of mind.

Megan smiled, clenching her teeth to keep them from chattering. Panic still swirled inside, but she forced herself to act natural. No way did she want Michael upset on her account. "Yes, thanks to you, I am fine. But what are you doing here?"

Mark glanced her way. "I could ask the same question. We're heading back to where we're staying. You?"

Megan shrugged. "Me, too. The mall was just a stop along the way."

Mark hunkered down by her car. "Can you fix it?" she asked. "I found the tire and a jack, but no wrench. I don't even know if the tire is okay."

"Mmm. Let's see." He glanced toward Michael. "Can you keep him out of mischief?"

"Sure, but I should learn how to change a tire."

"Yes, you should," Mark said, "but right now I need you to watch him."

Megan bowed formally. "As you wish my lord."

Michael giggled. Taking her hand, he pulled her toward the mini-van. "Let me show you my new game."

Megan followed his happy chatter with only half her attention as from the high seat of his vehicle, she watched Mark. "How old are you, Michael?"

"Seven. My birthday is April 18th. When's yours?"

"Next month."

"Daddy's is in March. But yours is coming right up. What you gonna do on your birthday?"

"I don't know. I haven't thought about it."

His eyes widened as though he couldn't quite believe that. "Oh. We'll have a party for you?"

"I don't know." Megan tried to let him down gently. "I don't know where you're going to be."

"We'd come where you are. We would. Daddy likes you." He lowered his voice as though sharing a secret. "I can tell."

Megan blushed. This had to stop.

"Megan." She jumped as Mark poked his head in the window. "The replacement tire isn't the right size. You should have had everything checked out before starting out on your vacation."

Anger flared, then died at his implied criticism. "I know. What am I going to do now? I don't want to keep you any longer."

He shrugged. "We're on no particular schedule, are we Bud." Reaching in, he rifled his son's hair. "More important, what is your schedule like? Are you far from your destination? We could take you there, and return to fix your car."

"I am not sure how much further it is. I was looking for the turn off on 7 to Five Geese Flying Lodge."

He stared. "Five Geese Flying Lodge?"

Michael bounced up and down. "That's where we're going. That's where we're going. You can come with us."

"You're kidding, right." Megan shook her head. Maybe God *was* in this.

"That's right. Any particular time of arrival?"

"After four."

"No problem, it's almost that now. Tell you what. I'll put on that spare. It will at least get us to a station if we go slow. You drive the mini-van."

Megan felt sweat start in her palm. "Me! Drive your car. Sheesh! I almost crashed my own."

He covered her hand with his. His grin reminded her sharply of his son. "But my tires are in great shape, and Michael will love the company."

A half hour later, driving the mini-van, she followed Mark in her car. It took another hour to find a place to repair her tire and, even then, Mark insisted on driving her car "just to be sure everything is all right."

By the time they reached the turn-off, the air was comfortably cool, the clouds were distant puffs and blue skies prevailed. After a few more miles, they turned off 7 into a narrow washboard path through the forest. The mini-van took the rough road in stride. Megan carefully kept to the center of the path/road, praying the vehicle wouldn't get scratched by the branches reaching toward them over the roadway on either side.

Several private roads led off from the main path to cabins buried deep in the wood. Almost at the end of the rough, winding road, the Five Geese Flying Lodge sign beckoned.

As Megan drove over the rise, the lodge, the condos, and cabins dropped away before her gaze. Beyond, the gray-green lake stretched to a haze of evergreen trees on the distant shore.

Michael pointed out the window, ""Look, the silver car."

"Oh, no," Megan said as she pulled up in front of the lodge a short distance from the sports car. Her gaze froze on the lanky blond-haired man swaggering from the lodge.

Getting out of her car, Mark hurried to her side.

At that moment the man looked up, stopped and leered. "I'll see you around, Babe."

"Oh, Mark," she cried, her face white. "What am I going to do?"

CHAPTER SIX

It is God that girdeth me with strength, and maketh my way perfect. Psalm 18:32

His hand gripped her arm, steadying her as she all but tumbled out of the mini-van. Reaching past Meg, he lifted his son to the ground. "Whoa, Bud. Don't want you knocking Megan over."

"Sorry," Michael said. "Can I run down to our sailboat, Daddy?"

"Well, all right, but you be careful. Don't go into the water or the boat."

As Michael dashed away, Mark returned her puzzled look with, "We come here every year. Before we arrive, Jay gets our boat ready for us."

"You come here every year. I thought the Salstrand reunion took over the whole resort."

"From what I understand, they did. Except for an upstairs condo, which I own."

"Oh. Why, did they sell one of the condos?"

Taking her arm, he helped her onto the wood plank

porch of the lodge. "Needed the money for repairs, I suppose. Rose and Jay Mays just bought Five Geese Flying Lodge a few years ago. Before they bought it, the lodge burned down, and the cabins had seriously deteriorated." He glanced around at the newly constructed lodge and refurbished cabins. "Been quite a change around here in the last couple of years. It just gets better and better."

"You've known them long."

"Jay at least. We come up once or twice every summer. I help Jay a bit, as well as vacation."

"What a deal," Megan said, going through the door he held open. Somehow, she had in mind that the owners of the resort were a comfortable older couple who bought the place for something to do in their retired years.

Mark led her toward the blonde-wood registration desk where a slender woman with shoulder length flaxen hair greeted her with a smile at Mark introduction.

"Rose, this is Megan West. Megan, Rose."

"Welcome. Your condo is ready and waiting." She laughed. "Before you ask, I don't have a key. But, don't worry; no one locks anything around here. Right Mark?"

"She's right." He answered Megan's skeptical grimace. "No crime here since the Mafia gave up on the lodge as a hide-out some sixty years ago."

"Mafia hang-out? You're kidding, right?"

"Not at all," Rose said. "Mark can show you the door where the owner back then kept track of things, like the first snow, etc."

"Interesting. Ah, shall I pay now?"

Rose waved a slender hand. "Whenever."

Taking her card from her pack, Megan handed it over. While Rose wrote up the receipt, she said, "Mark, call Jay. He'll want to know you've arrived. He's working downstairs."

She motioned toward the tree trunk on which a narrow stair wound down to where the floor leveled with the lake side of the lodge. On the other side, sliding doors led to a deck looking over the lake.

Mark stuck his head over the rail. "Jay, you down there?"

A chuckle sounded. "Be right up."

An athletic man, of medium height and with a trim mustache, emerged wiping his hands on his jeans. "Mark, just in time. They still haven't gotten the hot tub working yet. Could use your help once you settle in."

His amicable smile included Megan. Mark took the opportunity to make introductions. "Megan, may I introduce you to Rose's husband, Jay. Jay, Megan West."

At Jay's questioning glance, Mark's cheek twitched. "She's a guest, Jay. We met on the way up. Her car had a flat."

He made no mention of their time in Minneapolis, and Megan gathered he didn't want his friends to read more into our relationship than that of casual acquaintances. Of course, that's all it was. A pang of regret shot through her. Did she wish for more?

"Megan West." Jay spoke with unmistakable

sincerity. "I hope you enjoy yourself this week." "Mark, when you're ready, I'll be down there."

Jay disappeared down the stairs. Popped up again. "Say, where's that boy of yours?"

"Down by the lake." Mark walked over to the sliding doors and surveyed the docks. Frowning, he slid open the door, walked out onto the porch and leaned over the sturdy waist-high railing. "Michael. Get out of the water, and get your shoes back on."

Megan heard Michael say something, but didn't catch the words.

"No, you cannot go wading without supervision. Maybe I can get away later."

Sighing, he came back into the room. "I don't know Rose. Keeping tabs on that boy gets more difficult all the time." The twinkle in his eyes belied his exaggerated sigh.

"I...I could watch him for awhile." The offer slipped out of Megan's mouth before she considered.

"You sure? What about your family?"

"If you're going to be busy, I'm sure no one will mind if Michael tags along with me. I know we're supposed to meet for supper."

"Here," Rose led the way to the deck. "See. They're using that large tent down beyond the swimming area."

A large gray-white tent rose over the green grassy area next to a few scraggly trees by the lake. From the lodge, which straddled the sloping knoll to the shore, Rose pointed out the main attractions. The road curved down the hill around the left of the lodge to the docks below. The deck on the right overlooked the large grassy area set up for volleyball and croquet. Below, older children swung on the swings and zipped down the slide.

Cabins lined the space above the steep slope that enclosed the lower area. The wood cabins stretched off into the woods. Further up the slope, the condos rose two stories high. Beyond them, Megan recalled from the brochure, was a tennis and basketball court.

Pulling on his shoes, Michael waved to her. "Michael," she called, "Want to help me settle in?"

Megan had no trouble seeing his vigorous nod. Rose laughed, "I see you've made a conquest."

Megan contemplated her words as Michael showed her to her condo. On his part, Mark insisted on driving her car to its parking place and carrying her things inside.

"Yours is the middle one here," Michael said. Emulating his father, he politely opened the door for her. "There are three places on this side and three on the other. Well," he told her with a grin, pointing up, "actually they're up there."

"Which is yours?"

He pointed up to the right. "Up there. The one on the end by the basketball courts. Wanta play basketball? Daddy says I get to stay with you while he helps Uncle Jay."

"I didn't know he was your uncle."

"He's not," Mark said, setting down a load of

groceries on the counter. "I try to teach Michael to be respectful. That means, Bud," he said firmly, "that you call this lady, Miss West--not Megan."

"I know Daddy."

"I think that's it," Mark told her. "If you don't mind, I'll see what Jay needs." He hesitated. "If Michael gets to be too much, send him to the lodge."

Knowing so little about children of this age, Megan couldn't imagine Michael misbehaving. "He'll be fine, I'm sure."

Without a word of when she would see him again, Mark strode out the door. Not giving herself time to think about the unexpected pain his abrupt departure caused, she smiled, "Shall we put these groceries away first?"

With Michael's help, in a surprisingly short time, she had unpacked as much as she needed to at the moment. Straightening, she perused her domain. The one bedroom condo had a pull-out couch that she wouldn't need, an old fashioned heater, a cooking stove, a refrigerator, and a bathroom with shower.

After freshening up, Megan let Michael lead her toward the lake. "I can't go straight down the bank," she told him.

That stopped him momentarily. His forehead crinkled with confusion. "Why not?"

Megan touched leg. "My leg isn't as good as yours." She smiled as unpleasant memories flickered through her mind.

Michael continued to frown. "Why not?"

Megan managed, "I had an accident."

To her relief, that short explanation proved enough for the energetic youngster, who turned and race ahead of her down the road. She followed him out onto one of the docks, where all sorts of boats gently rocked back and forth. Michael pushed out his chest and pointed out his father's blue and white sailboat that rocked back and forth near a large blue pontoon boat. Further on, she spotted another pontoon boat, a red one, along with several worn fishing boats. A sleek speed-boat roared in a long curve around the lake, throwing up a bank of white waves.

Sitting down on the dock beside Michael, she followed him in taking off her shoes and dangling her feet into the cool water that lapped soothingly along the sides of the boats.

His bright chatter she found amusing, but also tiring. As the sun touched the horizon, she watched as first one, then another, then couples and small groups made their way to the tent. Megan reluctantly pulled her feet from the water and slipped on her canvas shoes.

"Hungry?"

Michael grinned and rubbed his stomach.

"Good." She didn't want to face her relatives alone. "Your father said you could eat with my family."

At his inquisitive stare, she added. "Relatives, you know. We're having a Salstrand reunion."

"That's not your name."

"No, but it was before I married."

"Married? Where's your husband?"

Stay calm, Meg. It's just a question from an inquisitive little boy. "He's dead." It sounded so final. Maybe she didn't cover as well as she thought because Michael slipped his little hand into hers. It felt surprisingly comforting.

"It's okay."

Megan stared across toward the tent a long time. Her feet didn't want to start the short walk down the beach to the tent.

"You don't want to meet them, do you? Is that bad man a relative?"

Not having spent much time around young children, his perception surprised her. He remembered the man who accosted her. "It's just. Well, I haven't seen them for a long time. Others I don't know at all."

"Like the bad man?"

"I don't know him. I hope he isn't here for the reunion." Her words trailed off as they drew closer, and a few individuals glanced their way. Megan found herself gripping Michael's hand.

"Megan!" A pleasant, matronly woman hurried toward her. "Megan, why didn't you tell us you were coming?" The woman hugged her and let her go before she could respond.

The welcome warmed something inside. "It was a last minute decision, Aunt Selma."

"Walfred. Come here. Megan's here."

Walfred's husky arms embraced her in a bear hug. "About time, Gal," he growled in her ear.

Megan blushed under his perusal. "I'm here now."

"So you are," he roared. Uncle Walfred never could tone down his voice.

He took in Michael who shifted back and forth from foot to foot. "And who is this? Yours?"

"Afraid not. I am sort of baby-sitting I guess." At the lad's grimace, she amended. "Michael is my new friend. I told his Dad he could join us this evening."

"His father?" Megan read all sorts of questions in her aunt's eyes.

"Mark Adrian. We happened to meet on the way here. He helped me change a tire," she explained. "Turns out he owns condo 6 and helps out the owners."

"I see," Selma said, but it was clear she didn't.

Linking her arm with Megan's, she practically dragged her toward the tent where the others gathered. Within a short space of time, Aunt Selma introduced Michael to some of her younger relatives. With Megan's permission, he dashed off with them, first to play, and then to eat.

"Now Megan, this is Dan and Elsie Salstrand. Megan West. Peter Hanson, (he's a doctor--never been married)," Selma added. Megan flushed under her aunt's all-too-obvious match-making. Megan could almost swear her aunt didn't breathe as she rattled off the list of introductions.

"Your second cousin, Megan. Ann over there is his sister--she's in college. Their siblings are Seth, Danielle, Amy, Jonathan and Cassie. Cassie and Jonathan are the twins playing with your little friend. Michael isn't it? The children's parents are over there. Yes there," she said when Megan turned her heard in the direction Aunt Selma pointed.

"The auburn haired woman with the baize slacks. Here's Uncle Bob, you remember him. He's one of our patriarchs. And there is Shirley who keeps the family genealogy on track."

Aunt Selma ran a commentary on those who lined up at the serving tables, filling plates with turkey, corn on the cob, an assortment of fruit and vegetable dishes and a selection of delectable desserts. Megan knew everyone had been split up into groups and given a night to provide supper. She wondered if she would be asked to help. Her aunt assured her she could help out on Monday night when they were scheduled to provide a meal.

"Don't worry about it. We're going simple--sloppy joes and chips, etc. We'll talk about it later."

Three lovely teenage girls sang a benediction for the food. "That's Chelsea, Jessica and Tanya, daughters of the tall, skinny man over there--Jeremiah Handly. He's a widower," she whispered significantly. "Those girls are as different as can be. They'd be a handful for a step-mother, I think."

Dusk hid Megan's red cheeks. She whispered, "Aunt Selma, I am not looking for a husband."

Her aunt's coy smile told her she did not believe Meg. Inwardly, Megan groaned. After she finished supper, she found herself approached by cousins who she hadn't seen in twenty years.

"We haven't been introduced." Megan turned to face a man with a shock of blond hair and cool blue eyes who gripped her arm. She gasped and jerked back her arm. "You're that man with the silver car, the one who..."

He interrupted, "To think we're related. What luck!"

Megan snapped, "From whose point of view?"

He laughed as though she'd said something witty. "By the by, I'm Dan and Elsies' only son, Bryce. Hear tell, they've spoiled me rotten with much too much money and freedom. Then again, can you blame them with a son like me?"

Megan rolled her eyes, her tone sarcastic. "They have my condolences."

He laughed. "Would it help if I apologized for my behavior? I'll admit to a bit too much to drink."

Somehow, Megan found it increasingly difficult to be polite to the arrogant man. "Drinking and driving don't mix."

"You sound like my saintly parents," Bryce retorted, his smile fading. "Maybe we did not hit it off so to speak, but we are cousins--distant maybe--but related nonetheless. Since we'll be thrown together this week, I suggest we at least try to get along."

He had a point, and she nodded reluctantly. Bryce's grin widened again. "I'll show you I'm not such a bad guy, Megan West." His smile held a dangerous charm and reminded her so vividly of Jack's smile that it sent chills up her back.

His fingers trailed her cheek, and she pulled away.

"Miss West," Michael's presence at her side as well as his surprisingly mature tone caught Megan off guard, "are you all right?" He eyed Bryce with distrust.

"Who's the bodyguard?" Bryce pushed Michael's shoulder. "Go away kid. The lady and I are talking."

Uncertainty flashed in Michael's eyes until Megan took his hand. "Thank you, Michael. It is almost dark, and I think it's time we head back."

Aunt Selma caught up with her before they got far. "Oh, you can't leave now, Megan. We're going to start a camp fire, and all get to know one another better. You can't miss that."

How could she disappoint her aunt? "Let me take Michael back to his father first," she told her, but did not reckon with the boy.

His eyes shining, he begged, "Please let me stay. Please."

Sighing, she all but capitulated. "We have to ask your Dad." Besides, her leg hurt, and she knew she needed to take something if she was going to keep going.

They didn't find Mark at the lodge, but Rose said, "They went into Remer for something or other, but I'm sure he'll be fine with you. Cell coverage can be spotty here, but you could try calling him."

Megan grimaced as she held up her phone. "I never thought to ask for the number."

Rose chuckled and rattled off the number, twice,

before Megon got it entered correctly. With a nod toward Rose, she tried to call, but it went to voice mail. She left a message.

Rose shook her head. "You are still on the property, and I'll let him when they return. Go on with you and do not worry about it. "

On his part, Michael, impatiently, clattered through the DVDs available under the entertainment unit in the corner while she chatted with the owner. Finally, she could no longer ignore the pain zipping up and down her leg.

"May I trouble you for a glass of water," she asked, fishing in her purse for an extra-strength pain killer.

By the time they returned, a bright fire leaped in the darkness. Insects snapped in the heat and zoomed in on the skin. "Thank you," Megan said with heartfelt gratitude when a cousin handed her a bottle of insect repellent. First she sprayed Michael, then herself. With a wave, he dashed off to sit with Jonathan. Megan had no choice, but to accept the chair, the only chair vacant, next to Bryce.

Soon she forgot him when Jeremiah started a story, which everyone added to one by one as they sat around the fire. The story grew wilder and wilder, and the younger set convulsed in laugher.

As the story ended and the hour grew late, mothers herded their children to bed. Others talked. She mainly listened. Even Bryce's presence ceased to bother her. What harm could he do here? She'd almost forgotten Michael until Jonathan's mother took him off to bed.

Michael tried to hide a yawn.

Guiltily, she got to her feet. Megan wasn't used to considering the needs of a child. Doubts about her abilities as a mother surfaced, but she shoved them away. "Come on Michael. Let's get you home."

He made no protest as she took his hand. Bryce also got to his feet. "I'll walk you to your place." His tone booked no argument.

"As you wish," she managed.

"Such enthusiasm."

"You tried to hurt Miss West," Michael declared. "Leave her alone."

"A miniature gentleman. Takes after his father no doubt." There was no mistaking his sarcasm.

Megan sensed Michael's hurt. Protectively, she tried to push ahead, but she was tired, her leg ached, and she wished she could go straight up the slope like most everyone else.

Bryce made no comment when she chose the long way around, but she sensed he thought she did it in order to prolong the walk. "Bryce."

Turning toward the lake he murmured. "Lovely night this. Look at the moon pouring down its silver light on the lake."

"It is beautiful," she agreed, stepping back from Bryce when he tried to put an arm about her. "I don't think..."

"I am not going to hurt you, cousin. Can't we just enjoy the sight like friends?" He held out a tentative branch. "I'm a pussy-cat when I'm not drinking."

God had forgiven her so much, surely she should forgive Bryce. "Friends. As long as you don't drink."

He grimaced. "Another teetotaler."

"Under the influence, your behavior was less than gentlemanly," she said dryly, starting back up the road toward her condo.

"Was I so dreadful?"

"I think you know very well that you tried to assault me."

"Assault is a bit harsh, don't you think? What's a kiss or two? I wouldn't really have hurt you."

"How was I to know that? Besides, I happen to believe that kisses should only be given in true affection, not passed around like candy."

The portico of the lower condos served as the floor of the decks for the upstairs condos that overlooked the lake. Bryce halted under the trees that towered above them like shaggy fingers pointing to heaven.

"Megan." Bryce's deep tones reverberated through her, and she felt herself responding to his charm as he alternately teased and deepened his hold on her.

Charming! How could she possibly be drawn in by this arrogant man who openly jeered his parents' Christian values? Jack, too, could be so charming. He, too, had this air of sophistication. This time, her eyes were open to what she had refused to see in Jack, a man who said and did whatever it took to get what he wanted.

Silently, she chided herself for automatically

categorizing Bryce with Jack. She scarcely knew Bryce. Part of her felt drawn to him, another part clamored *warning!!*

Mark cut the tentative bond Bryce wove around her. "Michael, it's time to come up to bed."

"Okay, Daddy." He dashed around the building to his home-away-from-home.

A moment later he peered over the rail. "Nite, Miss West."

Mark coaxed his son. "Thank her for a nice evening."

"Thank you. Had a great time."

Megan smiled up at the cherubic face lit by a rather dim porch light. "Thank you. I never had a little boy to spoil all by myself."

He chortled. "You can spoil me anytime, Miss West."

The back door to the upstairs condo snapped shut. Bryce murmured, "Now that we're alone."

He leaned down. Panic vied with despair, because part of her almost wished for his lips to touch her. No! She wouldn't be drawn in again. Footsteps sounded overhead and a deep warm voice pulled her back to reality. "I thank you also, Megan."

"Anytime, Mark. Anytime. Michael is very special."

"Yes he is," Mark agreed, "But he isn't the only one."

In the darkness, she blushed. Taking the

opportunity, she hurriedly said good-bye to Bryce, whose angry frown suggested he was less than pleased with this turn of events. Closing the door to her condo, Megan breathed. "Lord, help me. I am so confused. I don't even like Bryce, so why am I drawn to him? By the way, thank you for the rescue."

Going into the bedroom, she flicked on the light. Grabbing up her Bible that she'd unpacked, she sat down and opened it. "Lord, show me what to do."

Later the words and phrases took shape in her mind, and she got up to write them down.

I thought forgiveness brought release,
But now in His love I see,
Tis but the beginning,
Of what Christ has for me.

Problems do not go away,
But now He's in the fray,
Guiding and directing me,
All along the way.

Putting away her journal, she shut off the light and climbed back into bed. "Thanks Lord," she prayed softly. "Help me to be worthy of your love."

CHAPTER SEVEN

So then faith cometh by hearing, and hearing by the word of God. Romans 10:17

Early Sunday morning Megan awoke to rain pattering on the ground and dripping from the trees. Her scarred leg let her know it wasn't taking kindly to the weather. Throwing back the covers, she shivered as she headed to the bathroom to take a shower. Though the water pressure was not as she would have liked it, the warm water soothed her. Megan toweled herself dry and pulled on a robe before sitting down with a hair dryer and brush to fix her hair.

Megan chose to wear a red silk blouse over a long black skirt and dressed quickly, adding a warm shawl against the rain. In the tiny kitchen, she fixed herself toast and apple cider. Popping a pain killer into her mouth, she finished the small glass of cider. Megan glanced at the clock and grimaced as she hurriedly brushed her teeth before heading up the slope to her car.

Thankfully the rain let up, and she had little trouble

finding her way back to highway 7. Heading toward
Longville, she turned the opposite way from the way she
came in. As the miles passed Megan wondered if she had
somehow gotten her directions wrong. She told herself,
"Rose said it wasn't very far."

About the time she decided she'd gone too far, she
spotted the city limits sign. Megan looked for a church as
she slowly drove through the small town with its buildings
dotting either side of the road in a rather hap-hazard
fashion. Why hadn't she taken the time to program the
address into her GPS? Grr.

Except for the small, square sign, she would have
missed it. From the outside, the dark wood building had
little appearance of a church and the parking lot was
hardly more than a postage stamp.

Megan pulled the shawl more tightly about her
shoulders before stepping from the car. Peering through
the drizzling rain, she walked toward the most likely
building and opened the door to a ramp. Shedding her wet
shawl, she hung it on a waiting hook before heading up the
incline.

She heard singing and her insides churned. She'd
always hated arriving late, but as she entered the
sanctuary, she flushed when she found herself facing the
whole congregation. Her shoulders tightened, and she
glanced around only to focus on the smiling face of Mark
Adrian and Michael, who motioned for her to join them.

Her shoulders relaxed as she made her way down
the narrow aisle to sit beside Mark. Michael pushed

around them both to sit down on her other side. Megan flushed at the tantalizing thought of how well they fit together as a family. Did others think so, too?

Sensing her embarrassment, Mark squeezed her hand. "If we had known you wanted to come, we'd have picked you up."

Megan only had time to smile at him before the pastor had them stand to sing. Megan relished the familiar choruses, though they were sung slower than she was used to. Mark sang with a deep sincerity that made her quiver, while Michael sang with joyous abandon. The sincere faith of the small congregation surrounded her with the presence of the Lord.

Textured white ceiling and walls enclosed the unpretentious rectangular sanctuary with the ceiling vaulting over the pulpit. The design emphasized the stained, rough wooden cross of blonde-wood, which spoke eloquently of Christ's sufferings by the spikes nailed into the cross piece at either end. The American and Christian flags flanked the cross.

A large open Bible faced the congregation before the pulpit on the polished communion table. Globes of light hung from the ceiling, and fans slowly turned air, muggy with the moisture. Shades in green and brown covered the rows of windows on each side of the room.

After they sat on the surprisingly comfortable unpadded pews, the pastor introduced a representative of the Gideon Bible Society. The representative, a balding man in a worn linen-look suit and a busy green and mauve tie, acknowledged the pastor's welcome. As he opened his Bible, his gaze swept over the congregation.

In well modulated tones, he read Romans 8: 18-30. Verse 28 hit her anew. *"And we know that all things work together for good to them that love God, to them who are the called according to his purpose."*

A moment later she bowed her head as further on verse 32 spoke even louder. *"He that spared not his own Son, but delivered him up for us all, how shall he not with him also freely give us all things?"*

Every verse burned into her heart. Freely give? Could it possibly be true?

Leaning forward, she listened as she hadn't listened to a pastor in a long time.

"God cares," he said. "He cares enough to reach out to us. Oh the wonder of it all. All our answers are in God's book." He held it up.

"He is in control, so let God be God."

Megan searched her heart. Had she done that, let God be God, or had she diminished him by trying to earn his forgiveness?

Her disturbing thoughts drowned out the last of the representative's talk. After a few minutes, he sat down, and the pastor took the pulpit. He was a slender man whose gray suit matched his styled dark hair. A muted red tie enlivened his conservative suit. His ready smile and easy manner spoke of a man who cared about his flock.

Opening his Bible, he began with a prayer before launching into a topic that usually made her wince.

"Predestination," he said, "is a rescue and restoration operation. It means He stamps His image on us--to those who respond to His love. God already planned out where we'll be when He is finished with us. It is the provision of a loving, caring father. Predestination is only part of the plan." It was a whole new take on the subject.

He drew a picture of a God who loves so much that He seeks out His creation. He read Romans 9:15. ...*I will have mercy on whom I will have mercy, and I will have compassion on whom I will have compassion."*

"He took the initiative," he said. He went on to say that it could only happen by grace, "God's grace."

Nothing she could do made any difference, except one. "Predestination, he expounded, "is God at work. Co-operating with God is obedience..."

All her failures flooded her mind, her envy of Sam, her rebellion in marrying Jack, her slowness to give God control of her life. How could she open up all that was inside to His inspection?

The pastor spoke right to her, and she covered a gasp. "He is not taken by surprise...Jesus called personally and individually..."

A voice inside spoke with aching gentleness, *I love you Megan Salstrand West. I love YOU--not what you can do for me. You cannot earn my love, I give it freely. I love you. Will you not trust me?*

Gulping back tears, she felt Mark's hand tighten around hers. Not the crying type, part of her recognized with amazement this woman who cried so easily. "Yes,

Lord," she murmured, wiping tears from her cheeks. "Please, help me let down the barriers that still remain. Help me not just to know you as Savior, but also as Lord of all."

Megan hung her head. "Forgive me Lord for trying to come to you on my terms, not yours. Thank you for dying for me."

As the pastor closed with prayer, Megan reached into her purse, took out a tissue, and wiped her face. Michael's gaze held concern.

Smiling, she whispered, "I'm fine, Michael. Now, how about a smile?"

The tension left his little shoulders. With a grin, he bobbed up after the benediction. Megan and Mark followed him down the aisle to the front of the sanctuary, which also happened to be the back entrance.

Outside, Megan shook her head. "The 'front' entrance is at the back of the sanctuary, while the 'back' entrance is at the front." They laughed at the paradox.

"That's weird," Michael said. "Miss West, are you coming out to eat with us?"

The rain only drizzled, but the wind had picked up. Megan drew her shawl, which Mark found for her and placed around her shoulders, more closely about herself. "I don't know," she stuttered, blushing.

Mark chided his son, "Miss West probably has other plans, Son."

"No, not really." Again she blushed and wished her pale skin wasn't so revealing.

"Than you will join us?"

"Look," she said, wondering how to extricate Mark from an invitation extended by his son, "I planned on going back to the lodge and rest awhile. There is no need...." She glanced from Mark to his son and back again.

Mark appropriated her hand and grinned. "You still need to eat. Doesn't she, Bud?"

Michael bounced up and down. "Say yes. Say yes. Say yes."

Mark's widening grin told her, he sensed she weakened. "Would it help if I bounced up and down, too."

A gurgle of laughter dropped from her lips at the image. "Hmmm. Well..." She sobered, "Mark, this isn't really necessary. I know how impulsive children can be." Actually she didn't....

Seeing her hesitation, he assured, "Say yes, Megan. I want you to come." He ruffled Michael's damp hair. "Michael just beat me to the asking. We do want her to come, don't we, Son?"

He sounded so like his son, a nervous giggle again erupted. How confused and unreliable were her emotions these days. The drizzle of rain could have suddenly become buckets, and it would not have stopped the joy bursting forth inside.

"I'd love to come. You lead, and I'll follow."

His eyes sparked, then darkened. "I wonder," he murmured almost too softly for her to hear. "I wonder."

Puzzled at this change, she let him escort her to her

car. The mini-van waited a few cars away. Opening the door for her, he waited for her to get in.

"Wait until I pull out, then follow."

Megan nodded.

"Daddy, can I ride with Miss West. Can I? Can I?"

"May I," he corrected.

"May I, huh? May I, Daddy please?"

Mark halted this with a look. "Megan, would you mind?"

She exchanged a grin with Michael. "Not a bit. Get in Michael." She frowned. "Does he need a car seat?"

"We still use a booster, but he is big enough without one. And it is only a couple of blocks." Mark hesitated as though he, too, wanted to ride with them. Almost reluctantly, he closed her door. Leaning down, he peered into the window she lowered. "Buckle up, Son. Be good."

Michael readily promised as he squirmed around to find and attach his belt.

"All right, then. Megan, stay behind me."

She snapped a salute that made Michael chortle. "Yes, Sir."

Raising an eyebrow, Mark snapped back with a mock frown. "At ease, private." With amazing precision, he pivoted and marched off to his vehicle in perfect military style.

She glanced toward Michael as she started the car. "Was your Dad in the army?"

Michael puffed out his little chest. "Marines."

"I see." Putting the car in drive, she inched backwards, turned and followed Mark's mini-van back to the highway. It wasn't far back to the center of town, and she parked beside him in front of a small, seemingly the only, cafe in town.

Rough wood paneling darkened the dim interior, while the upper walls were dotted with wild animal pictures and large stuffed fish.

One teenage waitress in blue jean cut-offs and T-shirt, fluttered among the dozen or so tables that catered to a mixture of local and tourist trade, including several individuals from the reunion.

Choosing a table by the window, they waited for the busy waitress to bring menus. Michael's stomach growled, and he complained rather too loudly, "Daddy, I'm hungry. When can we eat?"

Mark flashed Megan a look of chagrin. "You have to be patient, Son." Glancing at her, he sighed. "Kid's are not known for their patience, I'm afraid, but I suppose you know that."

Megan's gaze held a question that took him by surprise. "I...I thought. Younger siblings? Nephews. Nieces. Baby-sitting."

The ache inside slammed anew, stronger than ever, and, while she tried to pass off her response lightly, her voice cracked with deep seated emotion. "I married young. No family. Little baby-sitting." She shredded her napkin, unable to hide the pain on her face. Silently, she chided herself for revealing so much, too much, to this relative stranger. Strange. She felt closer to him than she ever did to Jack. Megan shook her head to banish this dangerous line of thinking.

"It's all right, Megan. It doesn't matter. I was just making small talk. Married long?"

Thankfully, the waitress arrived to take their orders, and, by the time she left, Michael's questions and general chatter kept Megan from more personal conversation. Grateful for Michael's presence, she relaxed and enjoyed the leisurely dinner.

Michael plied her with questions that, coming from him, she did not mind answering. Somehow, every time she looked into his eyes, her arms itched to hold him close. She sensed that deep inside sadness lurked--and need.

"Are you married?"

"Not any more."

"Are you sort of divorced, like Daddy?"

My gaze jerked to meet those of his father. "Divorce...I thought...."

His lips twisted cynically. "She left us soon after Michael was born, though the papers were never officially signed." He sighed. "But she is dead."

"Oh." Megan didn't know how to respond. Michael waited for an answer. Licking her lips, she forced a smile. "No. No, I am not divorced. My husband died."

Mark's face softened. "I'm sorry. I forget other people have suffered, too."

Megan didn't want him to misunderstand, and she

sought a way to soften the judgments in her heart. Still, her tone sounded harsh to her ears. "Jack wasn't the model husband."

Getting up, she reached for her purse. "I really must be going." She nodded toward the receipt. "If you'll tell me how much I owe for the meal."

Megan couldn't stand sympathy. Mark put his large hand over hers where it trembled on the table. "I asked you to lunch. My treat, but don't retreat, Megan. Please."

She drowned in his gaze. "I...."

"Don't retreat from life because you've been hurt."

Wrenching her gaze from his face, she nodded curtly. "Thank you for dinner."

As she headed out the door, Michael's plea to his father nailed her heart, "Daddy, why is Miss West angry with us? Why is she running way? Doesn't she like us anymore?"

"Oh Michael," her heart cried, "I am not angry with you." But she could not turn back, not when her insides bled.

Mark's response laced the wound further, "She's not running from us, Son," he said sadly, "but from herself." From herself.... She heard a world of understanding in his voice.

On the way back to Five Geese Flying Lodge, tears flooded her eyes, and streamed down her face faster than she could mop them up. Gunning the motor, she drove without appreciating the green trees lining the road on either side, rising tier by tier to the overcast skies. The rain began in earnest as she turned off onto the dirt road to the lodge. It dripped off the trees onto the car roof and splattered on the ground.

At least, she thought parking the car and walking toward her room, *no one will notice my tears.* Megan rubbed her leg that ached from both exertion and the weather. Her pain-killer meds had run their course, and she took more before stripping off her clothes and pulling on a warm blue robe with red piping. Shutting off the lights, she crawled into bed and fell into an exhausted sleep.

Groggy with sleep, she awoke hours later, feeling almost worse than when she lay down. Her head felt stuffed with cotton, and her mood did not improve at the continued overcast sky. Splashing water on her face woke her to some semblance of rationality.

While dressing, she critically reviewed her day. What a display of emotion? What a fool she made of herself at the restaurant. She could see now that Mark meant no harm.

"Lord," she moaned, "I'm going to have to apologize, aren't I? How did her life get so complicated?"

Yet, facing herself honestly, she admitted she felt more alive than she had since she was a child. Yet, she wasn't sure she was ready to release the safe little world she had built around herself since Jack's death.

What about Mark? What did his attention mean? She had far more questions than answers, and she forced herself to concentrate on getting ready to meet with the family down by the lake.

Pulling on a light-weight, red, Nebraska Husker jacket over her jeans and black turtleneck sweater, she headed down toward the tent. Though the sky remained overcast, the rain had stopped, and a light breeze scented everything with pine and more.

The aroma of corn on the cob, chicken, and gravy wafted on the breeze and brought forth a deep rumble from her stomach. Thankfully, no one noticed either the sound or her tell-tale blush. Others found their way to the tent, and soon they lined up for the delectable and hearty meal.

Sitting down at a table with Uncle Walfred and Aunt Selma, Megan was soon drawn into discussion of what the family planned for that evening. Some continued to sit and converse while others went off to fish or swim. The younger set headed to the swings.

After they put up their plates, someone brought out the T-shirts sporting cartoons of the patriarchs of the family with Salstrand Reunion emblazoned across the front. Within minutes, most of the shirts had been exclaimed over and purchased. Holding hers, she overheard Peter call out, "You are all expected to wear your shirts to supper Tuesday evening."

Everyone laughed.

By the time she emerged from the tent, the sky had cleared of everything but the mosquitoes that dotted the sky and zoomed down on exposed skin. Delicate dragonflies swooped and turned in the air, and she cheered them on as they snapped up mosquitoes with each swift movement.

Bryce, who had been sitting at another table, approached. "How about a round of croquet?"

"Well..." Megan saw the field laid out not far from the tent.

"Come on, Megan," Uncle Bob encouraged. Of slight build, Uncle Bob drew others to him by his ready wit and humor. "If I can do it, a young thing like you should be able to manage."

Megan remembered his visit from when she was a child. She'd always welcomed his visits because they were joyful times. He always brought her a special little something and treated her with the respect of a doting great uncle. Guilt at ignoring him all these years brought a flush to her cheeks and an affirmative response to her lips. Another fence to mend.

While Bryce rounded up more players, she walked with Uncle Bob to choose her mallets. "Uncle Bob, I'm sorry."

He didn't let her continue. "I figured you had a rather bad time of it." He sighted down his mallet at the final stake. "There's nothing to forgive, Megan. Just want you to know, I kept those prayers going up."

Megan hugged him, and he returned her embrace. "Welcome home, dear."

"Thanks, Uncle Bob." Her heart warmed with his understanding. It lasted throughout the game, despite Bryce's attempts to finagle his ball close to hers. She lost, but it did not matter. At least, it provided an opportunity to leave gracefully without the unwanted attentions of her cousin. Unfortunately, he excused himself from the game and followed her toward the dock where she watched the shallow waves dance up and down far into the distance.

Ever since arriving, she'd gravitated toward the lake, which soothed something within her. Out on the lake, the sails of the white and blue sailboat billowed, and the bow dipped gracefully. Michael waved from the deck, hollering something she could not hear. Looking up, Mark also waved.

Grinning like a silly girl, she waved her arm above her head, wishing with all her heart she was out on the lake with them. On a nearby dock, Chelsea, Jessica and Tanya dangled their bare feet in the water.

Their voices drifted over toward her. "I wish that Mark would look my way," said one.

"I'd just die." Megan identified Tanya from her tanned skin and cap of dark hair. For sisters, the girls each had a distinctive look. Fair Jessica had long curly hair; Chelsea, olive skin and shoulder length dark hair.

Jessica sighed. "Isn't he hot?"

Tanya whispered, "Do you think he's interested in her?"

"Who knows," Chelsea answered, "just wish it was me."

Megan smothered a chuckle at the collective sigh. How young they sounded? Was it so long ago, she talked and acted just like that? Her cheeks burned.

Plastering a smile on her lips, and, much to their chagrin, she turned and greeted them. "Hi, girls. Nice evening, isn't it?"

"Ah, ya." They acknowledged her greeting with rather sheepish grins, well knowing she'd overheard their conversation. Stilling a giggle, she turned back. In the growing darkness, the water appeared dark and sinister, and she shivered, hoping Mark and his son would soon come in..

Bryce slipped up to her, and put an arm about her waist before she even knew he was there. From the girls emanated a whispered sigh.

"Wish I was as popular as *her*."

"Isn't Bryce handsome?"

"They make a nice couple, too."

Bryce grinned down at her. "Don't we though?"

Megan found it difficult not to respond to his charm. "But I'm not some silly teenager."

"Glad to hear it." The undercurrent made her uncomfortable, and she glanced toward the sailboat. Mark picked this unfortunate time to come in, and her gaze met his blazing eyes. Surely he wasn't jealous? She was woman enough to savor the thought, even while reason prevailed. His anger was more likely focused on Bryce for his earlier behavior.

Jumping from the sailboat, Michael threw his father a line before helping tie up the boat. Grinning, he dashed toward her. "Hi, Miss West." At Bryce's frown, his greeting trembled tentatively, and she slipped from

Bryce's loose embrace to kneel before the vulnerable child.

"Hello, Michael. Did you have a good day?"

"Yes. Yes," he said with a nod, "but we missed you. Why did you go away?"

She frowned, wishing Bryce stood further away. "I wasn't feeling the best," she faltered, hesitated, then added, "but I am fine now. Thank you for caring."

Unexpectedly, he wrapped his arms about her neck with such a grip she almost fell back into the water. "I'm glad, because...because I love you, Miss West."

"Here. Here." Bryce said, trying to untangle the lad. "You're dirty."

"Stop it, Bryce." Megan wrapped her arms about the little boy. "I love you, too, Michael."

"Michael," his father commanded with a decided chill in his tone, "Miss West is busy. You can see her tomorrow."

Megan glanced up expecting to find anger, but found only a sadness that rocked her. "I am never too busy for Michael," she told Mark, releasing the boy.

"Go on home, Son." He watched his son run up the slope toward the condo.

Glancing back at her, he said, "I don't want him hurt."

Indignant, she flashed back, "How dare you think I'd hurt that precious treasure."

Mark winced at her attack. "I think it best you stay away from him from now on."

He might as well have added, "and me too."

CHAPTER EIGHT

*Let the wicked forsake his way, and the
unrighteous man his thoughts: and let him return unto the
Lord, and he will have mercy upon him; and to our God
for he will abundantly pardon.* Isaiah 55:7

Had Mark socked her, Megan doubted the hurt
would have been worse. Bryce took one look at her face
and swore under his breath. Almost numb at Mark's
rejection, she let Bryce lead her from the dock, along the
sandy beach, to the bonfire flaring up into the night sky.

Megan slapped a mosquito as it landed on her neck,
then another. "Hope they have repellent over there again.
My protection is gone."

Beside her, Bryce murmured, "I'm all the
protection you need, Fair One."

Megan let that pass as they joined other family
members being drawn to the beckoning blaze. Bryce
brought up two plastic chairs and seated her with all the
attention she craved at the moment. Solicitously, he
sprayed her neck and arms and ankles to keep away the
pesky mosquitoes. He made no demands on her, offering

her only a sympathetic smile now and again that warmed her wounded heart.

Chelsea, Tanya and Jessica joined them, still talking softly. The younger set also came. Little Jonathan came up to her, his disheveled hair and a dirt mark across his cheek made him look like a smudged angel. "Is Michael here? Is he coming?"

"I'm afraid not. I'm sure you can find him tomorrow."

"Okay." The lad ran around the fire and plopped down onto the ground near his sister Cassie and his other young cousins. As other adults pulled up chairs, Chelsea started a ghost story that, in their turn, each child added to until they had everyone laughing.

The laughter died down to a silence where no one felt the need to talk. The fire snapped and glowed at Megan's feet, warming her legs and face. Dan threw on another log, and the fire flared up again, highlighting the pensive expressions on the faces seated around the fire. So many different faces, so many different lives, yet all drawn here by blood. No one forced them to come or to care about one another. They came, they cared, because they were related by a common thread of ancestry. Megan thought, *We have a bond that could not be broken--a blood bond.*

A blood bond. That's what she had with Christ as well. He gave his life for her. It did not matter what she did, He cared for her. "Thank you, Lord," she whispered, then began to sing softly, "Thank you, Lord for saving my soul...."

Others joined in, and they sang it through several times. Someone else started another chorus. Then another rang as the family members lifted voices in song. Jonathan and Cassie waited for a lull, then began, "Jesus loves me this I know, for the Bible tells me so...."

Yes, she thought, *Mark may not care about me, but Jesus does.* Somehow it helped ease the hurt of Mark's rejection.

A reflective mood fell on the adults, driving the children away to play elsewhere. Peter, a slender man with sandy hair, stared at the fire. "I almost didn't come to this reunion," he said, "but now I'm glad I'm did. I am grateful to be part of a family that has kept the faith through so many generations."

The reflective mood lingered as the fire slowly died, and one by one family members, individually or in couples, found their way back to their quarters. In the darkness, she heard mothers and fathers calling their children.

The twins' mother sounded harried. "Cassie, Jonathan. Cassie where's your brother?"

Cassie giggled. "Can't tell. I promised."

"We should keep our promises," her mother said. "Now Jon, come on out wherever you are."

"Boo. Here I am. Here I am."

"Come now. Time for bed."

"Aw. Do we havta?" Their pleas for a later bedtime faded into the distance.

Those around the fire exchanged understanding grins. Silence enveloped them. The trees whispered secrets, and the water lapped the shore behind Meg, lulling her to sleep.

She awoke to find Bryce peering into her face. "I think 'tis time for the princess to be abed." His solicitation held a lighthearted leer.

Jerking up her head, she felt her cheeks burn when she realized they were the only ones remaining at the simmering fire. "Oh, no. How late is it? Bryce, have I slept long?"

"Not too long. You're beautiful in your sleep, you know."

"Thank you for not deserting me."

He pantomimed a deep bow. "The prince awaits your every wish."

Laughing, he grabbed her arm and hoisted her to her feet. Too long idle, her leg did not wish to co-operate, and she all but collapsed in his arms. Surprise glinted in his eyes as he gathered her close.

Megan pushed away, "No, Bryce. I am not melting under your charm. My leg fell asleep."

He sighed, "How cruel, these mortals."

Megan could not help but respond to his light hearted banter. Together they sauntered along the beach to the road and on up toward the condo. The porch lights of the other condos somewhat dispelled the night, but Bryce stopped her in the shadow of the trees.

"Megan." He willingly pulled her into his embrace.

She felt the tug of his charm and found herself excusing his drinking, his abusiveness, his language.

Just like you did Jack?

Lord, what am I doing?

Megan pushed away. "No, Bryce. This isn't right."

His embrace tightened. "Megan. Princess. You came willingly enough. You want me. I know you do."

Megan pushed against his chest. "Bryce, let me go. Let me go or I'll scream."

"No, cousin. I don't think so."

She heard anger in his tone, felt it in the grip on her arms, and that too reminded her sharply of Jack. "Bryce, please let me go, and we'll talk...."

His lips ground down on her mouth. Choking at the abrupt assault, she began to fight in earnest as his hands began to roam.

The voice sounded low and deadly and *close*. "Let her go."

Bryce released her so suddenly she fell back against Mark who righted her with an impersonal chill. "I don't see what business this is of yours," Bryce told him. "It is not as though you treated her any better."

In the dim light, the two men faced each other. Tension crackled in the air.

"I don't assault vulnerable women," Mark said, "and I suggest you leave Megan alone."

"Not physically," Bryce retorted, leaning back against the tree trunk.

A muscle twitched in Mark's cheek. "I suggest you

leave."

"When Megan tells me to leave."

She managed to keep her voice steady. "Just go, Bryce."

"As you wish, Princess." With a mocking bow, he sauntered down the hill toward his parent's cabin.

Mark said nothing. Taking her arm he escorted her to her door. Opening it, he waited until she was safely inside.

"Mark?" she tried to break through the chill. "Why are you so angry at me?"

"I don't think this is the time to talk about anything. We're both tired."

"So you're going to shut me out. What about Michael? Am I just to ignore him from now on? What do you think that will do to him?"

"It is better than letting him get too close to you only to have you walk out of his life. I won't have him hurt that way." Just inside the doorway, Mark loomed above her. The lights in the living area picked up the pain in his eyes.

"Is it Michael that concerns you...or your own past?" The accusation came as much a shock to her as to Mark, who staggered into the room. The fury on his features twisted to a pain so deep, she caught her breath.

"Mark, who did this to you?"

"Listen Megan." Mark backed up toward the door. "I didn't mean it, about Michael. I won't stop him from seeing you, but how will he deal with saying good-bye?"

For a fleeting moment, she sensed this giant of a man, who was usually so self-assured, spoke of himself rather than his son.

"Do you think I have so many friends that I would not keep in contact at least by letter, phone or E-mail?"

Mark's face cleared. "He'd like that. He's quite a whiz kid on the computer."

"Good. Glad that's settled." She threw her shawl over the back of a kitchen chair, and straightened it out.

Still, Mark hovered in the doorway. "Why do you hang about with that jerk?"

"Bryce? He's my cousin. And sometimes," she told him, "he is more gentlemanly than others I could name."

The shot found its mark, and the large man winced. "I see." His lips tightened. "You'd prefer the company of a man who regularly assaults you. Fine!" With that he stepped outside, closing the door with a decided snap.

"Mark. Mark, I didn't mean...."

It was too late. Megan heard his steps clomping heavily up the outside steps on the side of the building to the upper level.

"Lord, what am I going to do about him? He is hurting so much. Does he really think I'll hurt Michael? Lord, please help me know what to do about both Mark and Bryce."

Petitions continued to fall from her lips as she pulled off her clothes and slipped on a warm nightgown. Picking up her Bible, she began to read until the confusion in her heart eased, and she was able to sleep.

The next morning, she awoke refreshed. Blinking her eyes, she focused her thoughts, remembering. The disagreement with Mark did not seem quite so hopeless in the light of day.

Getting up, she pulled on a pair of navy slacks and red flannel shirt that opened to a white T-shirt. Megan sorted through her clothes, stuffed them into a duffel bag and headed toward the car. Opening the door, she heaved the heavy bag onto the front passenger seat, slipped into the driver's seat and started the car.

The sun peaked through overhanging clouds, taking turns with the rain, which sprinkled down now and again. This time she drove confidently to Longville, and parked in front of the Laundromat.

Dragging out the duffel bag, she wished for a strong hand to assist her. A moment later, the burden lifted from her shoulder. Whirling she faced her grinning cousin.

"Bryce, what are you doing here?"

"Does it matter?" He spoke precisely, too precisely, as though searching for the correct words.

"No, I guess not."

"Laundry, I suppose," he said. "How about I help you get it going. Then we can scout out the town together."

"Well..." She debated silently. What could Bryce do in broad daylight in this small town? Besides, it would be nice not to be alone. She shrugged. "Sounds good to me."

Bryce helped her load the washer, then asked,

"Where's the soap?"

"Oh, no! I left it back at the resort."

Glancing around, Bryce headed toward the corner and a coin operated dispenser of cute little boxes of detergent. Unfortunately, it took more quarters than what she planned for the wash. "Don't bother," Bryce said, getting change for a five.

He fed in the quarters for several boxes, ripped them open, and poured the contents in the washer. Closing the lid, she set the timer and pushed the large red START button.

"I'll pay you back," she told Bryce as he took her arm and led her out onto the sidewalk.

"Consider it a gift. Dad has pods of money so no one will miss a five or so."

"Pods? You sound English when you say that."

"Didn't you know? Folks spent time in England, and I went to school there for several years."

Being somewhat of an Anglophile with an insatiable love of regencies, this perked her interest. "I'd love to go to England sometime. Did you see the Tower and visit museums?"

He chuckled at her interest. "So, I finally discovered something to interest my fair lady."

Megan laughed. "There are two countries I have always wanted to visit."

"Ah, let me guess--England and Sweden."

Megan pretended shock. "How did you guess?"

They laughed in comfortable companionship, and

she wondered why Bryce could not always be this charming gentleman rather than the lecher who sought to seduce her. Had not Jack been the same? Not exactly. Jack had never had the benefit of the education and travel that gave Bryce a polish her husband lacked when she married him.

Indulgently, Bryce escorted her to the gift shops where she wandered about, enthralled with all the local products for sale. When trying to decide what to buy took longer than planned, Bryce, twice, was kind enough to run back to the laundry to check her wash.

Later, she returned with him to put the clothes in the dryer that refused to fully dry the clothes no matter how long she dried them or how many quarters she fed into the machine. Bryce frowned and paced. Finally she shrugged. "That's enough. In this damp weather, they'll never dry. I'll lay them out when I get back to the condo."

Shoving the damp and therefore heavy clothes into the car, Bryce wiped his hands on his form-fitting slacks that showed off his muscular thighs. "Thank you, Bryce. I don't know how I would have carried that duffel bag." She smiled, "God does provide."

Grunting, he took her arm. "God is just a metaphor for people who put themselves out for other people."

Shocked, she turned to stare at him. "You don't really mean that?"

Mischief twinkled in his eyes. "Don't I, my little innocent?"

"Innocent. Hardly." His condescension stung. "I

am a grown woman who was married and lost a husband."

"And still afraid to love a man."

"Bryce." Her tone warned him, and he backed off.

"Sorry." He glanced at his watch. "I'm starving. Let's eat."

He led her toward the same cafe where she shared a meal so recently with Mark and his son. "Is there another place to eat?"

"In a town this small? I doubt it, but what does it matter? We're right here."

Reluctantly, she followed him into the dim room and sat down. Her gaze kept drifting toward the table where she'd sat the day before. It seemed a lifetime ago. Megan let Bryce talk while she choked down her hamburger and fries. Bryce ordered a dinner and took his time eating. Megan tried not to fidget and sighed with relief when he finally got up.

Across the street, down a long hall holding other offices and business, they discovered a new and used book shop. It was a small shop crowded with shelves until it was difficult to move around. Other books spilled out of boxes on the floor.

The dark haired, dark eyed foreign-looking clerk nodded as they entered. A few minutes later, he announced in heavily accented tones, "I have to go next door. If you need me, come and get me. Just ask for Chase."

Bryce and Megan glanced at each other and burst into laughter. "Only in a burg like this," Bryce derided.

"Oh, come on," she said. "I like it. Can you imagine anyone leaving their store untended in your city? We wouldn't do that even in Kearney. The crime rate is probably nil here, and they have reason to trust."

Bryce rolled his eyes. "If that is the only compensation for burying oneself in a hole like this, it isn't worth it."

"Must you be so cynical? You sound as though you didn't even want to come to Minnesota."

"I didn't," he said flatly. "But now..." He did not disguise the desire in his eyes.

The store closed in on her. "Let's go, Bryce. There isn't anything here I want."

"All right." He lingered until the clerk returned. Taking down a calendar, he paid for it.

Outside, she sucked in a deep breath. Scanning his face, she saw dissatisfaction and the first faint lines of dissipation on his features. "I'm tired, Bryce. Time I head back."

"Already? The day has just begun."

Trying not to reveal the sudden discomfort she felt in his presence, Megan told him. "I also don't want to leave the clothes long, or I'll end up having a load of wrinkled clothes. Probably have to iron half of them now."

Bryce let her go. As she pulled out of the parking space, she watched Bryce head down the street and wondered where he was headed. Thoughts of Bryce slipped into the background as she drove back, and her mind worried on the problem of Mark.

Driving onto the resort grounds, she saw Mark on the lodge porch deep in conversation with Jay. In the distance, she heard the excited yells and screams of children at play. Was Michael with them? Her arms recalled his hug and the way he felt in her lonely arms. When had the boy wound himself around her heart?

Megan began to see the wisdom of Mark's request. Who would be hurt the most, Michael or her? But as she had slowly been learning, hiding away from feelings or from developing relationships only kept wounds open, and made them fester.

Mark was wrong. She saw that, too. She saw it because of the healing taking place within her own life, healing that was slowly, but surely freeing her.

That night, she provided pickles and chips and olives and buns, which she ran into Longville to buy later in the afternoon. She helped Selma and Walfred and Ann dish out sloppy joes (one of her favorites) and brownies that she managed to resist.

Conversation buzzed about plans for later that night. Uncle Bob held up an arm for attention. "We're going on a tour tomorrow morning to the old Salstrand stomping grounds and homestead. Anyone interested, be ready to go by nine."

After filling her plate, she sat down with the three girls who, though they welcomed her shyly, ate without their usual chatter. Megan sensed her presence made them self conscious. Worse, when Bryce sat down beside her, the girls erupted into giggles.

Even though she sensed Bryce was, thankfully, not the least bit interested in any of the girls, he flirted with them outrageously. He had them all blushing and stuttering and fluttering. From the wink he sent her, she knew he did it deliberately. She didn't know whether to laugh or be angry.

He didn't give her a chance to know her own mind before he whisked her from the table down the beach. Above her, she heard a man clearing his throat and glanced up to find Mark glaring down at her in condemnation from the deck of the lodge.

Anger flashed in her eyes. How dare he judge her because she chose to spend time with Bryce? She certainly hadn't seen him extend himself in her direction today. Anger still simmered when Bryce asked her to go on a pontoon ride with him.

Throwing a glare of her own toward the deck, which she doubted Mark saw, she said rather too loudly, "I'd love to go for a ride. You're the first to invite me, and I've been dying to get out on the lake." Megan laid it on thick, and Bryce seemed delighted with her ready acceptance.

The polite gentleman when he wanted to be, Bryce handed her carefully into the red and white boat and settled her on the long bench at the back.

"Anyone else going?"

"Who needs anyone else?" Handing her a life preserver, Bryce made sure she fastened hers while he pulled another over his own head.

A tiger-striped cat jumped on board and tried to settle down for a nap. Lifting him up, Bryce tossed him roughly back onto the dock. Undoing the line, Bryce pushed the boat away from the dock before revving up the motor. It purred to a roar as he let it out.

Below them, the gray-green waves echoed the overhanging cloud bank that refused to clear. Surprisingly, the usual horde of mosquitoes were not out, and the evening took on a pleasant haze as she watched the shoreline retreat. The water slapped soothingly against the bottom of the boat.

The lake curled around numerous inlets and bays, stretching out for what seemed for miles. Away from the shore, the lake appeared a deep mysterious green. As they neared other shores, the lake darkened to marsh-like shallows marked with warning red striped posts.

Bryce toyed with the speed, going faster, then slower, grinning back where she sat as though hoping to get a rise out of her. Instead, a sort of calm stole over her. Megan felt in harmony with nature. She sent Bryce a serene smile that he returned with a very different smile. Even his teasing did not disturb her at the moment.

She turned her attention to the shore where simple A-frames alternated with palatial native wood mansions, and rustic cabins edged the shore along with the resorts. The various structures interrupted the continuous line of trees growing thickly to the edge of the lake. At times, the trees grew out from the land at such a steep angle their branches rippled like fingers in the water.

When his verbal jests did not rouse her, Bryce zigged the boat toward the warning markers. When she gasped, he laughed, and she fell silent. Observing his steady hand on the controls, she decided he was in complete control.

When he headed the prow toward the shore, she merely sighed. A few minutes later, he left the controls, sat down beside her, and put his arm around her waist. His grin riled her, and she firmly pushed him away. "Get back to the driver's seat," she told him firmly, resisting the impulse to respond with the hysterics he sought.

With a sigh, he returned to the wheel, but the look he shot her promised a reprise. Megan ignored him, already regretting her impulse to go with him. Actually, she didn't regret the ride; she regretted not insisting others come with them.

For a time, he geared up the motor, then slowed. Megan kept her eyes on the shore where trees backed each other row on row until they looked like mountains in the distance. The water turned dull gray, reflecting the growing darkness.

Bryce checked for lights, but found none, and she was sure he'd soon turn back. In the distance, she watched a blue and white sailboat skim the waves. She wished she was with Mark and Michael.

Nearer, a speedboat roared by so close the pontoon boat rocked back and forth in its wake. The rhythmic motion might well have lulled her to sleep, but for Bryce's bold gaze that kept her alert and wary.

They entered an inlet where the water smoothed to glass. Bryce slowed until the boat appeared to glide over the surface. The stillness was broken only by the slow rhythmic motions of a single canoe. Bryce pushed the lever forward, letting the boat pick up speed. He edged around an island to another bay.

Bryce pointed to a long building on the shore. "There's the supper club where we're all suppose to dine tomorrow eve. How about stopping now for something to drink?"

Megan eyed the steps leading up the steep slope to the restaurant. *No way!* The thought of Bryce at the controls after a couple or more drinks would have given her enough reason to refuse, even without the cramp in her leg.

Absently, she rubbed her thigh. "Not tonight. Besides, it's getting dark, and we have no running lights. Let's go back."

"Oh, all right," Bryce growled, then grabbed at the rail as water churned up choppy and white, and the boat rocked haphazardly.

Biting her lip, she refused to give way to the fear licking inside. "Keep us safe, Lord," she whispered quietly, knowing Bryce could not hear over the sound of the engine.

She felt only relief when Bryce turned the boat back into the lake. The ride had gone on too long for her taste. Megan covered a yawn with her hand. It would be good to crawl into bed tonight. For a time, she settled back to watch the shore growing darker with the coming of night. "Please let us get home before dark, Lord."

Maybe she dozed. When she again looked up, she did not recognize the shoreline. They moved slowly in a small inlet where Bryce further cut the motor, letting the boat glide toward an empty dock.

"Bryce, where are we? This isn't right." Megan wasn't alarmed, not yet.

Bryce only grinned and left his seat. Sitting down beside her, he stretched out his legs. "It's very difficult to get you alone, not with the hulk always around to snatch you away. This time we're alone. Just you and me babe."

"I'm not your babe, Bryce, and it's time we go back. It's dangerous to be out on the lake with no lights after dark." Alarm stirred.

He grinned smugly. "I have a confession. I brought a spot light aboard, just in case. We'll find our way home. If there is one thing I am good at, it's navigation."

"I don't care. I want to go back. Now." Her voice wavered, and he pulled her close.

"Such spunk. I like that." He leaned back again, but did not relinquish his hold on her. "Come on, Megan. Relax. Learn to have a little fun."

"This isn't my sort of fun, Bryce. We're going back if I have to steer this blasted thing myself." Megan tried to get up, but Bryce roughly pulled her against him.

She felt the soft cotton of his shirt against her cheek. Her leg twisted, and she cried out in pain. Panic settled deep inside. *Lord, help me*. That simple prayer brought a certain calm. If she could reason with her cousin, she might just emerge with her dignity, not to mention her virtue, intact.

Shifting his weight, Bryce clamped her against him. Scarcely able to breathe, she began to fight, but his strength pinned her. "Stop this Bryce. There is more to life than this."

He only laughed. "I was taught to go after what I wanted."

"You're problem isn't your wants, Bryce. It is your need."

That stopped, momentarily. "I need you."

"No, you need the Lord."

"Not that. I'm not so bad as to need God."

"You drink too much, and you hurt people. Have you forced other women as you are trying to force me? You need help. Christ can help."

"Stop playing games, Cousin. I don't need help like that. So I drink a little too much. Everyone does. As for you…" She knew the conversation was over. His lips came down on hers. His hands groped.

And she fought. Laughing at her feeble attempts, Bryce forced her head up. Fury glittered in his eyes. "I want you, and Bryce Salstrand gets what he wants."

His lips mashed down on hers bruisingly. Megan's stomach churned at his furious assault. Her life jacket kept him at some distance, and he tore it off.

As he threw her down onto the bench her calm crumbled into total and absolute panic. Raising her head, she screamed.

CHAPTER NINE

And now I beseech thee, lady, not as though I wrote a new commandment unto thee, but that which we had from the beginning, that we love one another. II John 5

"Ahoy there. Having trouble?"

"No trouble," Bryce growled, before recognizing in the growing dusk the sleek lines of Mark Adrian's sailboat.

Mark all but purred, "Miss West might well have a different opinion."

Releasing her, Bryce got to his feet. "Get out of here, Adrian. This is none of your affair."

"A woman's honor is my affair. Megan, you all right?"

Sitting up, she straightened her T-shirt with trembling fingers, pulled her flannel shirt closed and buttoned it to the neck. Tears gathered in her eyes. She felt dirty and exposed.

"I see you don't have lights. I guess Michael and I will just have to escort you back to the lodge."

Before Bryce spoke, Megan accepted. "Thank you Mark. I was worried about that." Turning away from Bryce's sullen expression, she smiled at the occupants of the sailboat. "Thanks for coming."

Much to his father's chagrin and Bryce's fury, Michael piped up, "We was worried 'bout you, Miss West, so we followed to make sure *he* didn't hurt you again." Michael left no doubt what he thought about her erstwhile escort.

Megan grinned over at the boy whose hair ruffled in the wind. "Thanks for being my knights in shining armor."

Michael frowned. "Huh!"

Chuckling, Mark motioned for Bryce to restart his engine. She overheard him tell Michael, "It means we came to the rescue."

The motor nearly, but not quite drowned out Michael's, "She shouldn't go out with him. He isn't very nice."

Megan couldn't agree more. Bryce, too, must have overheard for he muttered, "Brat kid."

On the way back to the lodge, Bryce refused to either speak or look her way for which she was profoundly grateful. If he had, she wasn't sure whether she would have cried or screamed at him. Why did she put herself in these situations?

Finally, the pontoon boat lumbered up to the pier where Bryce leaped to the dock, pulled in the boat, tied it up and headed down the beach into the darkness, leaving her stranded on the rocking boat.

Left on her own, she tried to stand, but the tussle with Bryce had wrenched her leg, and it buckled under her. Nearby, the sailboat slid gracefully into place. How she longed to ride the sleek vessel.

Glancing over, Mark remarked, "What happened to your date?"

Megan tired to keep her voice from cracking. "He left."

"So what's keeping you from getting out yourself." She heard derision.

"I can't," she choked, hating Bryce, hating Mark, hating men in general. Why had she thought for one moment she could have a normal relationship with a man-- or want to? They were all insensitive beasts.

"But don't worry about me," she retorted. "I'll make it somehow." Grasping the supports of the canopy over the bench, she heaved herself to her feet.

Steadying herself, she watched Mark leap from the sailboat and tie it up before swinging Michael to the dock. "Hey Buddy. I'll bet Aunt Rose would have some cookies for you if you asked."

Michael's face lit up. "Sounds good, Daddy." Poised to dash off, he halted. "What about Miss West. Is she comin'" too?"

"I don't think so. You go on. I'll see to Miss West."

"Bye Miss West," Michael called before dashing off.

"Thanks Michael," she managed, clenching her teeth from the pain in her leg. The supports dug into her hands as she struggled to step forward.

Even in the darkness, Mark perceived something was amiss. "Let me help you."

"Oh, go away," she all but sobbed. "You're all alike. Charming one minute and hateful the next. I hate you. I hate all men."

Anger, then concern, flared in Mark's face. Timing his jump to the rocking of the pontoon boat, he jumped aboard, causing the boat to tilt heavily downward under his weight. With a cry, Megan's leg gave way. Crumpling to the deck, she felt something hit her head.

"Megan." Mark's voice sounded in the distance. "Megan!"

***

In the background, a buzz of noises separated into anxious voices. "How is she? Should we try to get her to a doctor? Too late at night. Isn't her cousin a doctor? I'll get him."

Megan heard a frightened squeak in Michael's plea, "Daddy is she gonna' be okay? Daddy?"

Rose's softer tones landed soothingly on her ears. "We'll just have to wait and pray, Michael." She must be in the main lodge.

Jay's voice sounded in the background. "Here's another ice pack for her head."

Megan felt disembodied, floating, though she winced when the ice pack connected with her head. "Oh." Blinking, she opened her eyes and tried to focus.

Peter poked at her head. "It doesn't look too serious. A slight bump is all. Keep ice packs on it. I'll check it tomorrow."

Mark bent over her, his face a study of concern. "Megan. What happened?"

Her leg ached like fire, and she snapped, "I fell."

Before his concern, her stony front crumbled, and she began to weep. The harder she tried to stop, the worse it got. Years of hurt flooded out of her.

"Take Michael out of here, Rose. Jay."

Rose said, "If you need anything..."

"I'll call."

Somewhere a door closed.

Arms, warm and secure, enfolded her and held her, not like the fierce embrace of a lover, but like the comforting embrace of someone who cared. It only made the tears fall faster.

For a long time, she cried. Mark made no effort to stem the tide or to try to make things better. He only held her. At one point, he pulled her onto his lap, and she snuggled close like a lost child.

In time, the tears abated, and she hiccupped a couple of times. Her nose ran, and she fumbled for the tissue Mark handed her. Blowing her nose, she wiped her eyes. Still no one said anything as she lay against his chest, comforted in the large arms that held her so securely.

"I'm sorry."

"For what?"

"I said some horrible things to you."

"And I to you." Shifting her weight, Mark looked down into her damp face. "Want to tell her why you couldn't get out of the boat without help. Something was wrong, wasn't it?"

Again, she felt her eyes tear up and a sob dropped. Mark growled, "Did Bryce hurt you?"

Megan nodded. "Yes. No. My leg. I mean..." She bit her lip. How could she explain? Lying close to Mark's heart, feeling his caring, she couldn't bear his rejection when he discovered the truth, but she could not blame it all on Bryce.

"He hurt your leg?"

"Yes, but...you see..." Suddenly it spilled out--all about Jack, the accident, the horrible scar and how unreliable her leg was. Throughout, she dared not look at Mark.

When she fell silent, he put his hand under her chin and forced her to look at him. "That's why you had some trouble on the stairs at the entertainment center."

Megan nodded, trying to look away, but Mark would not let her. "Your husband, he rejected you because of it?"

Again she nodded. She shrunk back from the glare of rage in Mark's eyes. "Your husband was a fool, Megan. A fool who did not appreciate, nor deserve, a wonderful woman like you."

Mouth open, she stared at him until he laughed. "Close your mouth." He sobered. "And you thought that I would reject you because of that scar?"

"It is ugly."

"But you're alive, Megan. At least you're alive. Be thankful for that."

Megan recalled that his wife was not. Did he love her still? "You were so angry with me," she said, sounding to her ears pettish.

"I don't like seeing you with Bryce. He's bad news. Jay and I saw him in town last night, drunk as a skunk, and not a nice drunk either. We practically had to hog tie him to bring him back here. Not that he appreciated it, and I doubt he remembered this morning."

"I didn't know. Sometimes he can be so nice. And he is my cousin, though distant."

"Keep it that way." He fingered her head. "Distant, I mean. How you feeling now?"

She smiled, feeling the corners of her lips droop. "I have a roaring headache."

"I was afraid you had a concussion. Still might. I want to take you back to your cabin." Setting her down, he got up. "Stay here. I'm just going to get Michael, and tell Rose and Jay we're leaving."

Megan was more than glad to lay back and close her eyes. Moments later, or so it seemed, Mark and his son reappeared. Though she protested, Mark wrapped her in a warm blanket and picked her up. While Michael held the door, Mark carried her outside, down the steps to deposit her in one of the carts used to haul equipment (and the help) around the grounds.

The three of them squeezed into the seat with Megan stuck in the middle. Mark ordered, "Lay your head on my shoulder if you feel at all dizzy." With a murmured and heartfelt, "Thank you," she complied.

Mark pulled right up to her door. "Now, Michael. Open Megan's door, then run up to bed. I'll be up later."

"Okay Daddy." As though sensing the seriousness of the situation, Michael made no argument, and, as Mark carried her into her condo, she heard Michael's feet pounding up the stairs.

Switching on the bedroom light with his elbow, Mark deposited her on the end of the bed. He pulled down the covers, took off her shoes and made her lie down. Covering her up, he tucked the covers under her chin. "Just like I do for Michael," he said with a grin. "Now, is there anything else you need?"

Megan tried to shake her head, but the attempt made lightening zip through her brain, and she groaned instead. "I'll be fine," she told him. "Just need a good night's sleep."

"I will check on you tomorrow, so don't be in too big a hurry to get up. If you need me..." He frowned. "Where is your cell?"

Megan felt a moment of panic. "In my purse..."

"I'll go check the boat." He touched her shoulder. "Don't move. Wait here."

"Sounds good to me," she managed. Megan heard his heavy footsteps fade down the hill outside. She wasn't sure how long it was before he squatted beside the bed.

"Here's your purse and cell phone. Let me give you my number."

"I, ah, yes. Rose gave me the number—because of Michael—the other day."

"All right then. But cell coverage isn't the best. I want you to get help anytime." Taking her cell he entered a number. "That will get you to the lodge. If you need anything—call." She nodded—slowly.

"Would you mind," he hesitated, "if I pray for you?"

Megan blinked back tears. "Would you please? And Mark, I don't hate you. I don't hate you at all."

"Good. Say you'll go out in the sailboat with me tomorrow afternoon, if you're feeling better? About three."

"I'd like that."

"Good." With that he bowed his head and began to pray.

Drowsily, she heard his prayer, deep with conviction. Amen. He leaned down and brushed her cheek with his lips. "Good night, Megan." He snapped off the light. A moment later, she heard the front door close softly.

Cradling the phone in her hands, she whispered, "Thank you Lord for Mark."

She wasn't ready yet to put a name to the warmth in her heart for the gentle giant.

CHAPTER TEN

The wicked watches the righteous, and seeks to
slay him. Psalms 37:32

She awoke to the sound of eggs and sausage frying.
Megan touched her head, wondering if she had been hit
harder than she thought. Throwing back the covers, she
staggered to her feet. Her head spun dizzily, and she
plopped back onto the bed. Only then did she glance down
at her grubby jeans and shirt she'd worn all night.

Aunt Selma popped her head in the door. "You
awake?" She bustled over to the bed, touched Megan's
face. "How are you feeling this morning? That nice Mr.
Adrian dropped by to tell us you'd had a nasty fall."

Megan tried to smile, but failed. "The dizziness is
beginning to pass now."

Selma steadied her as she stood. "There now, how
is it?"

"Hurts like everything." Megan made light of her
awkward position. Here she was, away from home, and
something like this had to happen. Her heart hardened
against Bryce.

Selma interrupted her less-than-charitable thoughts.

"I'm fixing a good solid breakfast for you."

"Smells delicious, but you shouldn't have."

"Now. Now. It's the least I can do. Glad your young man knew to come get me."

Megan rubbed her leg, which also still hurt. "He's not my young man, Aunt Selma."

"So you say, Megan, but he was pretty concerned about you." She got out Megan's robe. "Here now. Get into this and come to the table."

"I need a shower."

Her aunt nodded. "A shower will make you feel better. I'll be right here, should you need help."

"Thanks Aunt Selma." It felt good to be fussed over. The dizziness, too, had more or less dissipated. Other than a pounding headache and an aching leg, she didn't feel all that bad. Taking the robe, she retreated to the bathroom. Aunt Selma was correct.

A shower did make her feel better, and a couple of pain-killers helped dull the pain in both head and leg. By the time she emerged from the bed dressed in a red textured V-neck pullover and slacks, set off by a wide black belt with an intricate gold buckle, Megan felt almost normal.

Her hunger also returned and, much to her aunt's delight, she did full justice to her hearty breakfast. "Oh," she said, remembering. "I hope I didn't make you miss the tour."

"Actually no. Everyone slept in, and there's still time to go." She glanced at Megan sharply. "Are you thinking of going?"

"Yes. I'd like to see the Salstrand homestead again. I remember staying up those narrow steep stairs and using a very cold chamber pot." Aunt Selma chuckled at Megan's grimace.

"I don't think you should over exert yourself. At least, that's what Peter said when he dropped in earlier."

"I can stay in the van most of the time. In fact, it might well be more restful than staying here."

"All right then. But, Megan, you have to promise to take it easy." Selma bustled about, cleaning up the dishes and putting things away.

After her aunt left to find Walfred, Megan found a jacket and went to join the tour. Curious stares turned her way as she walked up.

"Are you all right, Megan?"

"We heard you hurt yourself."

Megan shifted uncomfortably under their sympathy. Uncle Bob gave her a hug. "Feel good enough for the tour?"

"I wouldn't miss it."

"Good. You'll ride with my daughter and me in her van." By the time everything sorted out, both vans had a full complement of passengers. Megan was relieved to note that Bryce was nowhere about.

The vans carried equipment that enabled Uncle Bob to give a running commentary to both vehicles.

Heading south, they skirted Brainard and continued further on south to a small country cemetery surrounded by fields. Along the low fence, a thin line of gently rustling trees surrounded the place where some of her relatives lay buried. Yellow and white wild flowers softened the utilitarian fence.

Already feeling tired, Megan stayed in the van and looked on from the half open window, while the others walked solemnly around the small rounded stones.

"Look at this."

"I didn't know Great Aunt Sofia was buried here."

As the group drifted further away, she only heard the murmur of their voices.

The cemetery showed evidence of care not only of a caretaker, but also of relatives. A variety of rose, white and yellow flowers dotted the site. One headstone had a large red sign tucked in the grass reading simply DAD.

Tears stung her eyes at the loss it signified. How she missed the counsel of her own wise father. Hurriedly, she swiped at the tears, glad she was alone in the van. "Oh, Lord, forgive me for not heeding Dad's loving advice about Jack...and other things. If only I could talk to him now."

I am your Heavenly Father. Megan sensed a still small voice speaking. *Talk to me. I will always listen.*

In the quiet of the cemetery, another block of healing clicked into place as more of her guilt over her past fell away. Leaning back, her heart soared with hesitant joy. She didn't even care how long the others took. In fact, she dozed off.

When Selma opened the door, the cool breeze

woke her with a start. Selma smiled knowingly. "Hope the
nap helped," Aunt Selma said quietly as Walfred helped
her into the van.

Megan nodded. Soon they were once more on their
way. Someone from the back mentioned the need for a
bathroom break. The others readily agreed, but there was
no place to stop.

Reaching a tiny town with nothing more than an
unused church building and a general store, Uncle Bob
told about playing baseball in the field with the cows.

"Guess what we used for the bases," he asked with
a deep chuckle. "Cow patties, of course." His arm sweep
took in the area. "I went to school and church here."

At the store, everyone but her piled out and into the
store. Megan took one look at those uneven cement steps
and automatically rubbed her sore thigh. Selma returned
laughing. "The only facility is a snake infested path out
back."

No one hazarded the ancient facilities. After a
picture taking session, they traveled on. Again, Bob took
the microphone. "My best friends lived at that farm.
And..." He continued to relate interesting bits and pieces
of his life.

By the time they stopped in Little Falls, Megan's
stomach protested. Hers wasn't the only one. They finally
stopped at a restaurant where the staff set up a long line of
tables. In a relatively short time, they sat down for large
portions of whatever they ordered. Megan shared her large
portion of cheese sticks with both Ann and Selma.

"Time is getting on, Dad," his daughter said. "We aren't going to have time for everything. You know we have to be back in time to get ready for supper."

Others too voiced concern. So, in the interest of time, the make-shift tour did not stop at Lindbergh State Park, but continued south to another cemetery and more relatives. By now, Megan almost regretted coming along. She had no idea it would take so long, and every part of her screamed for a nap. Her head ached, and she longed to lay down. Another part of her longed to be out on the sailboat with Mark, letting the languid waves provide a certain rest.

From the back came the murmur of voices, and Bob punctuated her dozing with his stories and memories. She murmured to Bob's daughter, "I need to get back."

"I do too," she said. "We'll have to do something."

Taking a quick poll, they found everyone in their van, except Bob, was more than ready to return to the resort.

At the second cemetery, when it became evident that Bob and some of the others would not be hurried, his daughter announced, "Our van is headed back. Who wants to go back with us?" They exchanged Bob for someone from the other van who also wanted to return.

As soon as they got back, Megan hurried down to the dock only to find Mark waiting impatiently for her. "I'm sorry," she heaved. "The family tour took much longer than I realized."

Mark handed her into his boat. "You should have

stayed home and rested."

"I didn't do anything," she retorted, "but ride and talk and doze. Trust me; I did not over exert myself."

"Umm." Mark got in beside her and sat down by the motor.

"Where's Michael?"

"Off playing with some of your young relatives."

As he fiddled with the starter, she leaned back, letting the sun that emerged from the clouds wash over her with its radiance. The sky cleared rapidly and the breeze stilled to a mere whisper, leaving the lake glassy smooth.

"I feel I could skate on the surface," she said, breathing in deeply. "It is so beautiful this afternoon." The sun on her forehead soothed away the last vestiges of her headache.

Mark frowned. "I don't much care for it. I know you don't know this, but this is abominable sailing weather."

Setting the rudder, he put her hand on it. "Think you can manage this while I try and start the motor?"

"Motor?"

He laughed. "As still as it is, the only way to get out where there is some air currents to fill the sails is to use the motor." He shrugged at her. "So I am not a purist."

Megan laughed. "Fine by me. What I don't know about sailing would fill volumes."

As Mark shoved the ship from the dock, she watched a school of sunfish scatter in their wake, their tails flashing in the light. "Umm," Mark growled, pulling on the cord. Nothing happened. Again he jerked on the cord and again nothing happened.

Languidly, the small vessel drifted toward shore. "No. No," Mark growled, impatiently trying to start the stubborn motor. "We're headed toward the mud."

Grabbing the rudder from her inexperienced hand, he tried to steer clear, but to no avail. Within moments, the sailboat mired in a patch of sucking mud--too close to shore to pick up a breeze and too far out to wade back.

"Ahoy there," Mark hailed a speedboat, which sped so close waves lifted the ship. They cut their speed.

"What's the problem?"

"Stuck. Motor won't work. Would you give us a tow?"

Chuckling, the deeply tanned young man threw a line. "Get a real boat."

Mark took his good-natured jibe in stride. "When you run out of gas sometime...call."

The young man laughed heartily. "I take better care of my motor than that."

Megan sensed Mark restrained a retort. Instead, he thanked the rescuer, who gunned his motor and left with a wave. "Any time."

After tying up at the dock, Mark began checking the motor in earnest while she sat in the silence, enjoying the moment. Water lapped against the side of the boat, rocking it gently. In the distance, she heard a speed boat or two. Excited voices rose and fell from the children swimming further along the shore. Leaning back, she let her eyes close.

"Megan. Megan wake up." Mark's hand on her shoulder jerked her awake.

"Ah, what? Where? Did I fall asleep again?"

"Looks like you needed a nap."

"I'm fine now." Stretching, she grinned. "Ready to go out?"

"Sorry to break a promise, Megan, but that motor needs some serious repair work. I'm afraid they'll be no sailboat ride today." Taking her hand, he assisted her from his boat. "Sorry," he said again. "I'll see what I can do."

"That's all right," she began, but Mark was already heading toward the lodge.

Uncertainly, she waited on the dock, confused by Mark's behavior. Anger flared momentarily, but at herself. She knew Mark was not like Bryce, so what happened? What had she done?

Discouraged, she started back to her condo when Mark caught up with her. "Megan, where are you going? Why didn't you wait?"

Seeing her troubled face, he said, "You thought I just went off and left you, didn't you?"

"Well, I...I wondered how I'd offended you." She felt a trembling start somewhere deep inside.

His arm felt warm and secure around her waist. "Offended me? Oh, Megan, when are you going to realize how much you mean to me--and to God?"

"You did leave."

"Yes." He escorted her to her door. "But only

momentarily. I was going to try for a speedboat, but they're all spoken for. I should have told you. Sorry."

"Apology accepted." In front of the condo, he pulled her into a loose embrace. Even though she'd never felt so warm, she shivered.

"Umm." His cheek brushed hers. He smelled of lake and open air, and, more faintly, of some intoxicating after shave.

The chatter of an approaching couple broke the spell, and Mark pulled back. She felt bereft. "How about it Megan? Will you join Michael and me at the Supper Club this evening?"

She hesitated. How she wanted to be with him, but the Salstrand clan was also gathering at the club.

Mark used his most persuasive bait. "Michael would love it. He hasn't seen you all day, and he's still worried about you. Come and you can prove to him you've recovered."

Oh, surely the relatives would understand, she rationalized. "I'd love to come."

"Great." Brushing a light kiss on her cheek, Mark left her alone.

Unsteadily, she managed to slip into the room and plop down on the couch. Gingerly, she touched her cheek. "Lord, when did it happen? I tried so hard to keep him out. When did I start loving Mark Adrian? And, what am I going to do about it now?"

For some time, she contemplated the newness of her discovery. Love, deep, strong and sure had taken root inside. Megan thought she loved Jack when she went against all she knew and believed to marry him, but this, this wasn't a feeling. It was so much more.

She didn't have much time to consider this new state of affairs. Getting to her feet, she headed to the bedroom to pick out something to wear. She didn't have much to choose from since she'd packed only washable things. She, however, had brought one dress--just in case.

Stifling a yawn, she lay down for a couple of minutes. The day had worn her out, and the evening stretched long before her. The thought of changing clothes depressed her, but she would not embarrass Mark. Not embarrass....

Laughing voices outside her window woke her, and she glanced at the clock. Thankfully, she had not overslept. She had not meant to sleep at all, just rest her eyes.

Pulling her new dress from the closet, she laid it on the bed while she hurriedly cleaned up and carefully applied a minimum of make up (especially blush to give some color to her pale cheeks).

The black rib-knit turtleneck hugged her body, while the snug waist and long skirt set off her petite figure. It felt warm and comfortable, yet gave her a feeling of elegance. Around her neck she fastened a long, gold-mirrored pennant and added matching earrings. The mirror told her she'd pass muster.

Picking up her purse, she transferred her essentials into the gold handbag she hung over her shoulder. One more pat to her hair, and she went to answer the knock at the door.

The admiration in Mark's eyes when he and Michael stepped inside more than repaid the effort she'd taken to dress up. He was devastatingly handsome in gray slacks, a shirt open at the neck and a blue vest--a look echoed by his son.

"Ready, Miss West?" Michael bounced up and down. "Ready to go eat? I am so glad you're coming with us. Will you sit by me?" He chattered excitedly, while Mark took her hand.

"You look terrific," he said, his voice quiet and deep.

Her heart pounding, she stammered, "Th...Thank you." A faint flush stained her cheeks. To cover her confusion, she leaned over to speak to Michael. Her face was all-too revealing, and she had no intention of letting Mark know how she felt about him.

"I've missed you today, Michael, and am honored to have supper with you and your father."

Glowing, Michael reached up and put his little arms about her neck. He whispered in her ear, "I love you."

She held him close. How she loved this little boy! How she ached to be there for him always.

"Michael, don't muss Miss West, too much." At the odd note in Mark's voice, she released Michael, and looked up to find a strange longing in his eyes.

He hid it under light-hearted banter. "Come, let us

depart, my dear."

Inclining her head, she stepped out the door and took his arm, while Michael reached for her hand on the other side. "Lead on."

Outside, the sky had once more clouded over and the air had chilled considerably. The light breeze broiled into a hefty wind, blowing leaves from the trees and tumbling small branches across the grounds. The usually placid lake splashed white-capped waves against the boats, causing them to rock and strain at the ropes holding them.

The air smelled heavily of moisture and damp earth. Shivering, she stumbled in the face of the wind and would have fallen if Mark had not pulled her close. "Michael, run to the car. I'll bring Miss West."

"I didn't know the wind was so strong," Megan tried to catch her breath.

With Mark's arms about her, she made it to the mini-van without falling over. Picking her up, Mark settled her in the vehicle. Slamming the door, he walked around to the other side, the wind billowing out the sleeves of his shirt. He slid inside and glanced over at her ruefully. "Whew! You all right?"

"I'm fine, thanks to you...again."

He glanced toward the lake. "Sure hope no one is out there tonight."

Original plans called for those at the reunion to take the pontoon boats over to the supper club. Megan sent up a silent *Thank you* they had changed their minds due to the length of the tour. God did work in mysterious ways.

Taking a comb from her purse, she repaired the damage to her hair. Thankfully her style was simple. In the mirror, she caught the twinkle in Mark's eyes.

"Won't do much good. We have to get out again at the restaurant."

Wrinkling her nose at him, she threw the comb back into her purse. "You're right."

"I doubt with this wind the rest of the Salstrand clan will be able to use the tent tonight. Wonder how they'll manage."

Guiltily, she stared out the window. "Well, truthfully, they all have reservations at the restaurant."

He glanced at her sharply. "I didn't know. I didn't mean to take you away from your family."

"It's all right. They'll understand--I hope." She giggled. "At least Chelsea and Jessica and Tanya will."

"Who are they?"

"Three young teenage girls."

Michael piped up. "They think you're adorable, Daddy. I heard them. They sounded so silly. What does adorable mean?"

Mark actually blushed, and Megan answered. "They think your father is very handsome. And they're right," she added, feeling heat redden her cheeks.

He grinned. "I begin to understand."

She fervently hoped not. What possessed her to be so frank? Nonetheless, his lingering gaze warmed her to her toes. She was glad when they pulled into the parking lot.

Michael jumped out first while Mark came around to help her down and into the front door. Mark requested a table overlooking the lake. They sat in the growing dusk, watching the wind bend the smaller trees and the white-capped waves crash.

In small groups, her relatives (all in their reunion T-shirts) found their way into the restaurant and on into the banquet room set aside for them. Feeling more and more uncomfortable, she blushed and smiled as they glanced her way.

Selma came over. "Megan, we expected you to join us." Megan heard her aunt's disappointment.

"I know Aunt Selma, but...."

"I'm afraid it's all my fault," Mark said. "I didn't realize this was a big night for the reunion when we asked Megan to join us."

Selma patted his arm. "Well, at least she is in good hands. I wonder...?"

Uncle Walfred peered over her shoulder. "What's this? Megan you belong with us."

"Hush," his wife said, "she's on a date."

To her embarrassment, Uncle Bob joined the debate. "This isn't where we're supposed to meet. What is everyone doing over here?"

Walfred roared, causing heads to turn, "She's on date."

Megan felt her cheeks burn. This was worse than being a teenager on her first date. "Aunt Selma?" It came out as a wail.

"Hush Wally. Leave the girl alone. She's an adult and can choose how to spend her time."

"She came to the reunion, and she belongs in there." He glared down at Mark. "Now young fellow...."

Uncle Bob interrupted, "You will all join us. Michael, isn't it?" he addressed Mark's son. "Wouldn't you like to sit with your new friends?"

"Sure would." He turned pleading eyes toward his father. "Can I Daddy? Can I?"

Mark looked at her. "It's your call, Megan."

"Do you mind?"

Walfred roared, "Come on. Come on." Selma sighed.

"All right," she told them, "we'll join you if you're sure."

Uncle Bob winked at her. Lowering his voice he said, "I wouldn't be a bit surprised if he ends up being part of the family."

Seeing the twinkle in Mark's eyes, she knew he'd heard. She wanted to sink under the table. Instead, she followed the line to the banquet room where the others good-naturedly settled around the tables. Even those from the tour had finally made it back. With everyone else in their T-shirts, she felt rather awkward, but Michael had no qualms. One of his young friends made a place for him, and Michael slipped in beside him.

Mark and Megan found a place at a small table across from Peter and Jeremiah. Across the room, Bryce, sitting next to Ann, glared. She turned away.

"Mark, this is Peter Hanson and Jeremiah Handly, the father of those three girls." She pointed out the three teens, who stared from her to Mark with envy painted across their faces. "Peter, Jeremiah, Mark Adrian. His son Michael is over there."

The slender Jeremiah chuckled. "So you're the wonder my daughters have been sighing over."

Megan flashed Mark a grin, finding him speechless. Peter broke the ice. "You own the blue sailboat, don't you? I've been considering buying one."

Conversation took off then, and the meal proved to be a time of laughter and fun and companionship. Bryce glared, but he was easy to ignore. Prizes were awarded for a variety of silly things from who had caught the largest fish to who had traveled the furthest to attend the reunion.

The evening finally broke up with a round of hugs for those who planned to leave the next day. Outside, they found the wind had abated somewhat, and the trip home meant only that she would soon be parted from Mark.

At the lodge, Michael jumped out of the van. Seeing the tiger-striped cat, he ran off after it. "Michael, don't go far," his father warned. "You know the rules."

"Okay Daddy."

Shaking his head, Mark helped her from the mini-van before escorting her to her door. "I had a nice time, Megan."

"I'm sorry about Uncle Walfred and Uncle Bob." She felt the heat of her cheeks.

Mark merely chuckled. "I like your relatives, with

one big exception."

"Bryce. I know. You know, after I married Jack, I always thought my relatives shut me off. That is, except for Aunt Selma. She made a real effort to stay in touch. Now I realize I shut them out. I was ashamed of what I'd done in marrying against my folk's wishes." Megan swallowed. "Jack had no use for sentiment or, as he said, 'encroaching relatives.'"

As though sensing she was not ready to go in yet, Mark led her to the picnic table in front of the condo. They sat down on the edge. "Why, Megan? Why do you shut people out?"

"At first, I guess I felt hurt that my parents didn't accept Jack." Her laugh sounded sarcastic to her ears. "I thought they didn't understand, but I was the one who didn't understand. I walked away from everything they taught me."

"Was he worth it?"

"Hardly!" Again the depth of her bitterness surprised her. The darkness provided a safe cover, and she found herself replying without checking every word. "I told you how he was, what he did. He died in the arms of his mistress." She gulped. "I kept that secret and blamed God, myself. I don't know. I couldn't bear how the family might look at me. Then my folks were killed. The pain." Megan gripped the table edge. "I couldn't deal with the pain."

Mark looked up at the stars dotting the sky between the tall pine trees. "Bryce is a lot like your Jack, isn't he?"

"How did you know? I don't want to be drawn to him, but sometimes...then, like Jack.... How could I be so stupid again?"

Mark's arm encircled her waist. "You are not stupid Megan. I confess I hate seeing you with Bryce. I don't trust him, and I worry about you."

Her surprise echoed in her expression. "Truly?"

"Don't you know?" Leaning down, his lips touched hers. "You are a very special person, Megan West. I'd begun to think your kind of woman didn't exist anymore."

His tender kiss shook her. Gulping, she confessed. "I'm just a confused woman who is slowly...but surely," she said firmly, "finding her way with God's help."

A smile touched her lips. "This trip has done that for me. God is speaking. And this time, I'm listening."

For a long time they sat in comfortable silence before Michael returned, and Mark took him off to bed. He kissed her gently.

A moment later, his face hardened. "How I wish Venessa...." She heard him mutter under his breath.

Shocked, she watched him leave. "Venessa? Lord, who is Venessa?"

She limped into the condo. The evening suddenly seemed cold and unfriendly.

Taking off her dress, she flung on a robe. "Lord, thank you for this revelation. As much as it hurts, at least I won't seek something from this relationship that can never be. But I hurt, Lord. I want someone to hold me. I want a child to love." She sighed. "I love Michael and his father so much."

For all her brave words, her heart felt lacerated. When sleep refused to come, verses flashed in her mind like a movie projected on a screen.

Take my yoke upon you, ... and you shall find rest unto your souls. For my yoke is easy, and my burden is light.

Finally, she got out of bed and knelt beside her bed. "Lord, I'm tired of bearing my burden all alone. I don't know why you put this love in my heart, but I give it back to you. Jesus, may your will, not mine, be done."

A peace soothed her heart, and a certain joy bubbled up inside. "Thank you, Lord. Thank you, Lord. Thank you."

Crawling into bed, she fell immediately asleep.

CHAPTER ELEVEN

The LORD is my light and my salvation; whom shall I fear? the LORD is the strength of my life; of whom shall I be afraid? Psalm 27:1

Megan slept late the next morning. After she finally got up and dressed, she took her toast and juice outside to eat at the picnic table. She also carried her Bible, which she opened before her on the table, along with her diary journal.

The peace of the night before had not evaporated.

Even the weather mirrored the new calmness of her soul. The sun smiled down out of an azure sky. The breeze merely whispered, gently eddying her hair. Insects buzzed and darted among the trees as though playing tag. Looking toward the upper deck, Megan grinned at the tiger-striped cat languidly surveying his domain from a comfortable lawn chair.

Flipping the pages, she came across Psalm 46. *God is our refuge and strength, a very present help in trouble...* She read on, the words undergirding her in a new way--

especially when she reached the first part of verse 10, which she quickly memorized. *Be still and know that I am God:....*

Be still and KNOW that I am God. In the cool of late morning, she did indeed know the deep stillness of God in her own life. It was as if right there, the healing, which began on her trip North, was coming to completion. Not that there wouldn't be problems yet, but the deep searing wound had scarred over.

"Oh, Lord." Tears flowed. How weepy she'd become, but it was a good, cleansing cry.

"Megan, what's wrong?" Sitting beside her, Mark put his arm around her. "What happened?"

"God happened, Mark. For the first time, I feel really healed inside. It feels so good." She laughed through her tears. "Oh Mark, I wish you could know this peace I have inside."

She sensed a stillness within him, a hesitation as well as curiosity. "How do you know I don't?"

"Sometimes I see such sadness in your eyes." Megan clamped her hand over her mouth--too late. "Mark, I'm sorry."

Taking her hand, he laced his fingers through hers. "You are a very observant lady. God has given me so very much, but, like with you, some things take a long time to heal. It would help if I didn't blame myself so much."

"Your wife?"

He nodded. "She left me, and it was partly my fault. She didn't marry a businessman from Kansas, but a lawyer with a bright future, a high lifestyle and money--all the things she so desired."

"What happened?"

"God finally caught up with me. Everything I worked for was so empty and useless. As for some of my cases, I felt I was living a lie. I was, in essence, lying--using every trick in the book to get off wealthy criminals."

He squeezed Megan's hand so hard she bit her lip to keep from crying out. Her heart broke for him. How she wanted to be there for him as he had for her when she poured out her heart about her marriage.

"Two things happened. I discovered my wife was pregnant and that she planned to have an abortion without telling me."

At her gasp he shook his head, his eyes dark with remembered pain. "On top of that, my mother called to tell me that my father had just been diagnosed with cancer and was not expected to live."

"Oh, Mark. How awful."

"Yes, but it brought me to my knees. Unfortunately, I moved too fast for Venessa."

"Venessa, your wife?"

"Yes." The knowledge relieved her mind. So there was no other woman in his life--that she knew of--Megan reminded herself sternly.

"I flew to Salina to see my father." Mark shook his head. "I thought it would be for the last time, but you know what? God healed him. The doctors did surgery and there was still cancer until God stepped in. I never believed in miracles until then. I was so excited I flew home and dumped all my renewed enthusiasm on my wife."

"She wasn't pleased."

"That's putting it mildly. Furthermore, Dad and I discussed my taking over the store, and I agreed. I was more than ready to come home and raise my family in a more secure environment than New York offered."

"The abortion?"

Mark looked away, the muscle in his cheek working overtime. "She insisted it was her right. We argued and argued about it." Mark choked, "I didn't want her to kill our baby, but I didn't know how to stop her."

"My enthusiasm, my overwhelming her, my demands, drove her away from me. She wanted the bright lights, the money, the status. At first, she held having the baby over my head as a way to keep me in New York. Then she lost interest in me altogether. It all happened so quickly." He paused for so long, Megan thought he was finished.

A moment later, he continued. "She, ah, wanted out of the marriage. She said she was in love with someone else--a rich, powerful man." Mark shook his head. "I didn't even handle that well. I told Vanessa I didn't believe in divorce and that was that."

"She didn't like that, I suppose." Megan didn't much like this woman or what she had done to this wonderful man who spewed so much hurt.

"Strange, I've never shared all this with anyone,

Megan. It is such garbage. And I brought so much of it on myself. If only I'd been more patient with her. By the time I got wise, it was too late. She wanted out of the marriage and motherhood.

"She was far along and even the *thought* of an abortion was horrifying. She could not understand that while an abortion would kill our child, it could well be dangerous for her as well. So, I went along with her scheme. She agreed to have the child and turn him over completely to me, if I didn't contest the divorce."

Megan felt tears on her cheeks. "Mark. I am so sorry. How could she not have loved Michael?"

"I don't know. I thought once she held that little bundle in her arms, her maternal instincts would take over." His face hardened. "I don't believe she had any."

"You took Michael and moved to Kansas."

"We've had a good life. I healed for the most part."

"And Venessa?"

"She lived high and fast. I prayed for her, but now it's too late. She died in a plane crash a year ago."

How she understood the pain of self-guilt. "Mark, listen to me. You must stop blaming yourself. That's what I did, for too long. I'm just learning myself, but God forgave me for my mistakes, my rebellion, all of that. He forgave me. It took me long enough, but finally I understood there was no way I could make up for all that I did. I have to trust that what Christ did on the cross, he did it for me without reservation. If he didn't, if I still need to earn my way somehow, His death wasn't really necessary or complete. You must accept Christ's forgiveness, and then forgive yourself."

Mark cleared his throat. "Oh, Megan. You are a precious gift." Again, he cleared his throat. "Thank you."

Getting up, he half smiled, "God and I have some things to take care of. We'll have a long talk while I go into town to find parts for that motor." He started off, turned. "Would you mind watching Michael until I return? I know he'd like that."

"I would too."

The look Mark sent her took away her breath. "I'll send him down."

A few minutes later, Michael burst down the stairs. "Hey, Miss West, Daddy says I getta spend the day with you."

"That's right. Hope that won't be too boring for you."

"I wanta spend it with you. I do. I do!" He bounced up and down

They spent time playing video games and board games, and she listened to his busy chatter as they walked.

He sang a ditty that made her laugh. She responded, "Want to hear a poem I wrote?"

His eyes widened. "You write, like in books and stuff?"

"Yup," she answered.

He bounced up and down. "Tell me. Tell me!"

Catching his hand, she quoted solemnly,

In Winter when I run outdoors,
Ice crackles beneath my feet,
But not as much as when I slip,
And ground and bottom meet!

"Again. He giggled. She had to repeat the verse until he had it memorized.

When his stomach growled, she fixed left over sloppy-joes and chips that they ate outside. With her permission, Michael fed part his meat to the tiger-striped cat that joined them, hoping for a treat.

"Wish I had a cat," he said wistfully, "but Daddy says there's no one to take care of pets at home."

"Maybe a dog outside?"

"He's too busy with the store. Gramma has a cat though. I play with her sometimes, but she doesn't like kids much."

Anger stirred. "Your grandmother?"

"No, she's great. Her cat ain't." He laughed. "I rhymed. I'm a poet."

"You're a poet and don't know it," she told him making him laugh harder.

Throwing his little arms about her neck, he strangled her in a hug. "I wish you were my mother. My real mother didn't love Daddy and didn't want me. Why didn't she love me? You love me, don't you, Miss West?"

Her arms held him tight. "Michael, I love you so very much."

"I love you, too. Why don't you be my mother? I

know Daddy likes you. You can marry him, and we'll be a real family. Please say yes, Miss West. Please." His pleas broke her heart.

"Michael darling, it's more complicated than that. You can't ask for your father. Marriage is a very serious step." She hugged him again. "But no matter what happens, I'll always be your friend. That won't change."

Quickly, she steered the conversation toward safer ground, and soon had Michael laughing again. Nevertheless, she saw the desire mirrored in his eyes when he looked at her. How could she tell him that his desire expressed the traitorous longings of her own heart?

Megan knew Mark cared for her, but enough? Was there a chance for the happiness she'd missed by running ahead of God's will? She had reaped bitter fruit.

"Lord," she whispered, "if there is to be a next time, I want to be sure, very sure it's right."

Later on in the afternoon, Mark returned and Michael ran off to him. Megan heard Michael cry, "Dad, you're home!" Then, "Listen to this poem Miss West made up." From her vantage point, she watched Mark lift his son into the air and hold him tight. Was it imagination or was there a new peace on Mark's face?

"He can stay with me now, Megan," Mark called. "I'll see you later."

Megan waved and went into her condo. Picking up her pen, she wrote down the words that had been chasing each other around her mind most of the afternoon.

I want to be a servant, Lord,
Sold out to thee,
Not letting desires take the place,
Of what you did at Calvary.

I want to keep my focus
On You and You alone,
To lay aside rebellion as
I kneel before Your throne.

Lord, keep me looking upward,
Help me listen to what you say,
Bathe me in Your presence
Each and every day.

Megan finished with a large AMEN, for it was the desire of her heart. Whatever happened with Mark, she wanted it to be God's will not just for her, but for Mark as well. This time she loved enough to let go.

CHAPTER TWELVE

*Give ear to my words, O Lord, consider my
meditation.* Psalms 5:1

That evening Mark and Michael accepted Megan's
invitation to join the Salstrand clan around the campfire.
Michael dashed around the circle and plopped down
beside his new friends. Mark sat down beside Megan on
the blanket she'd spread on the ground.

The look in his eyes as he slipped his arm about her
shoulders reawakened feelings she thought long dead. He
stirred longings in her she had not felt since Jack. But this
was more than feelings, more than sweaty psalms and
weak knees. What she had thought was love back then
paled beside the depth of what she felt for this giant of a
man beside her. In ways, his pain matched hers, but what
she felt was more than empathy. She knew that too.

Before she thought to shutter her thoughts, he read
them in her face and in her response to him. Even without
the exchange of words, they grew close in the darkness
around the glowing campfire with a host of others looking

on.

Uncle Bob started some crazy song in which they all joined in. Peter began another, and pretty soon everyone contributed a song, a ditty, a joke, an anecdote or a story until they all collapsed with laughter. Even the kids joined in, and Michael and his friends rolled on the ground, giggling.

As the night chilled, Mark pulled Megan close. It seemed the most natural thing in the world to lay her head on his shoulder. Smiles widened knowingly, and, she sensed, with approval. Much to her embarrassment, Aunt Selma actually nodded, and she wanted to sink into the sand when she heard the rumble of laughter in Mark's chest.

Unlike Jack, Mark fit right in. More, he seemed to like her relatives. That was more than she ever could say about Jack. With an inner pain, she recalled the first (and the last) time Aunt Selma and Uncle Walfred came to visit.

Jack stomped around their small apartment. "Meet your Aunt who? Forget it. I'm not meeting some old biddy."

"They'll stay at a motel since we don't have room for them here."

"I have no intention of dancing attendance to any of your relatives, Megan. I married you, not that bunch of do-gooder relatives, so just leave me out of this."

He stomped out, and she hadn't seen him again for three days. Even now the shame of covering for him made her sick inside. It wasn't the last time she covered for him.

Mark's breath tickled her ear. "Don't get too far away, Megan."

His warm caring gaze studied her face in the flickering light of the fire. "Are you all right?"

Megan nodded, but a shiver gave her away. "Jack," she murmured. "I was thinking of Jack."

She read questions in his eyes as well as hurt. "You're so different," she told him quietly. "So different. Thank you."

His grin lit up her heart. "Thank you, Megan."

From across the fire, Ann, her blond hair glowing in the firelight, sighed, "It is almost over, isn't it? Day by day more leave. In a couple of days, everyone will be gone."

A pensive silence fell over the group.

"Hello everybody." Bryce's voice sounded loud in the silence. He dropped a couple of packages on the ground.

"Bryce, careful," admonished his mother, coming into the light, "we don't want the crackers to crumble." She motioned toward the three girls whose arms overflowed with marshmallows, chocolate bars and more graham crackers. "Come Chelsea, Jess, Tanya let's pass these out."

The children left their antics at the edge of the circle. She heard Michael's cry with the others. "S'mores."

"Can I make mine?"

"And me?"

An older child asked, "Don't we need sticks to cook the marshmallows?"

"Right here." Peter dumped a load on the ground near the fire. Megan hadn't seen him leave.

"First come, first served." Uncle Bob grabbed a long stick, jammed three plump marshmallows onto the prongs, and held it over the fire.

Laughing, the children, who knew him for a soft touch, gathered round. Those first marshmallows went into S'mores for the kids. Michael was right in line with the rest.

"I should help Michael," Mark said, starting to get up. "I don't want him making a pest of himself."

"Don't worry about him. They love him. He's almost as charming as his father." She choked. "Oh, my." Her cheeks reddened, and she was grateful for the darkness.

Settling back down, Mark chuckled. "I see. I think I rather like the description. How about I fix yours, at least?"

Glancing toward her, Bryce's eyes blazed with fury. Grabbing a bag from the arms of a surprised Tanya, he walked over and handed them to Mark. The two men glared at each other, and Mark's arm tightened about Megan's shoulders.

Bryce muttered, "Meg, I need to speak with you."

Secure in the circle of Mark's embrace, she felt no threat. "Go on." she said. "I'm listening."

"Not here. Not tonight."

"When then?"

"Tomorrow. I'll take you out in my speed boat."

Mark overheard. "Right. So you can take her to some secluded inlet. I think not."

"Stay out of this. This is between my cousin and me."

"I don't think...." she started, but he interrupted.

"Listen. What happened before? I'm sorry, but you have to give me a chance to hear me out. I promise not to try anything. Or isn't forgiveness in your vocabulary?"

"Right." Mark dripped sarcasm. "Thrice shy and all that."

"Megan, I don't give up easily."

"Be quiet, both of you and let me think." His accusation stung. Around the campfire, others roasted marshmallows and ate S'mores. Faces showed traces of sticky white and dark chocolate. Why had Bryce ruined this pleasant interlude for her? Yet, he needed the Lord, and this might be an opportunity to witness about her new-found joy.

Megan thought about his attempt to kiss her when her car broke down, and his assault on her during the pontoon ride. She also thought of Jack. As though a veil lifted, she saw her own vulnerability. How could she even contemplate being alone with this man?

Slowly, she shook her head. "Bryce, you need the Lord, and I would love to share what I know about him. Yes, I will go on that ride with you...."

Mark shook his head, his eyes unbelieving. Bryce's face widened into a predatory grin. "All right, Cousin. We'll have our own little revival out on the lake."

Megan shuttered at the lust lurking in his eyes. "But," she added, "I will not go alone."

Bryce stiffened and a smile twitched Mark's lips. "I'll be happy to chaperone."

"I'll just bet you would," muttered Bryce. "Megan...."

"Bryce, I would be a fool to be alone with you. If you want to talk, fine, but not alone."

"If you don't trust me," his hurt sounded so genuine she felt herself weaken.

She whispered, "Lord, help me be strong."

Lifting her head, she heard a new firmness in her tone. "No, Bryce, I don't. The choice is yours. The ride and the talk, but only with someone else present."

"Forget it then." He shot to his feet. "But you'll be sorry. I'm used to getting what I want."

With a sense of misgiving, she watched him melt into the darkness like some demonic spirit. The confrontation left her weak, and she was more than happy to let Mark fix her a S'more.

How do you like your marshmallows?"

"Burnt to a crisp."

"Ah, a girl after my own heart." His attention diverted her troubled thoughts.

He bowed toward her as he presented his offering, a graham cracker sandwich squishing with burnt marshmallow and melting chocolate. Giggling, she ate it with relish, Giggled as he fumbled with his own. She ate one and Mark, three more, before they called it quits. Laughing ruefully, he sat down and wiped away the last traces of chocolate and sticky marshmallows from her cheeks. His touch sent shards of warmth all the way to her toes.

The others, too, were satiated. Little by little the others drifted away, their conversations merging with the whispering trees. The fire burned lower when no one added any new fuel.

"Dad," Michael said, "Jonathan wants me to stay in his cabin tonight. Can I? Can I please?"

"May I, Son."

"May I?"

The other boy pleaded, "Please, let him."

The boy's mother, a slender woman with auburn hair, laughed. "It's fine with me, if you agree. We'll be leaving the day after tomorrow so this would give the boys more time together."

Mark nodded. "You have my permission then, but...." His words halted his son, all ready to dash off. "Don't forget your manners, and behave."

As they moved off, he glanced toward Megan. "I hope I made the right choice. It is so hard to know these days."

"You worry about him being abused. I don't think you have anything to worry about."

"I don't mean to insult any of your relations, but

you never know. You hear so much on the news."

"I know, and I am not insulted." Gingerly, she touched his face. "I think you're a wonderful, caring father. Fact is, you remind me a little bit of my own father."

Memories subdued her. "If only I'd listened to him. If only I had not caused him such heartache. Mom, too."

Mark held her close. She felt his heartbeat drumming rapidly, before realizing it beat in time with her own. "Megan, remember what you told me. God forgives. He has forgiven you, and so, I am sure, did your parents."

For a long time, they talked beside the dying fire before he escorted her back to her condo. For a moment, she thought a shadow edged from tree to tree, but when Mark made no comment, she decided it was only her overactive imagination.

Nonetheless, Mark sensed her unease. "Are you concerned about Bryce's threat?"

"It does bother me"

"Me, too," Mark said. "I suggest you put a chair against your door during the night."

"You don't think he'd be that brazen?"

"I don't know what your cousin will do, do you?"

Megan shook her head. "No. Actually, I don't ever recall meeting him before. I might have, when we were kids, but if so, I don't remember. I don't trust the man."

Taking her hands, Mark held them. "Let's pray about it."

My heart thumped and tears sparkled in her eyes.

Her heart's desire had always been that Jack, that her husband, would be the spiritual leader of the home. If she hadn't loved Mark before, she did now.

"Please." Humbly, she listened to his prayer. The depth of his relationship with God embraced her as well.

When he finished, she sniffed. "Mark. Thank you. You make me feel so safe."

The memory of Mark's good-night kiss lingered long into the night. But, it didn't quite drown out Bryce's ominous threat, and it was a long time before she slept.

Megan awoke to a strange scraping at the door. She'd heard the wind rising, and, for a moment, she thought it was simply the wind blowing something against the door. She heard it again. The chair. It moved. Throwing back the covers, she hurried to the door. Bryce's frame blocked the exit. A boyish smile etched his face as he surveyed her from head to foot.

Even though she was decently covered in a long, warm nightgown, she felt stripped before him. Her heart tripped with fear. "What are you doing here, Bryce?" She tried to sound confident, but both of them heard the waver.

Again the smile. "The boat ride, remember? I promised you a ride."

"And I turned you down." She felt safer now. He was her cousin after all.

"You don't understand. No one rejects Bryce Salstrand."

"Well, I did. Now get out."

He shut the door.

"I'll scream and everyone will come running."

"I don't think so. The condo on either side of you is empty or don't you recall the couple in number one left late last night? Uncle Bob's daughter left yesterday, and that takes care of the other side."

"Above."

Bryce slapped the ceiling affectionately. The place is unusually well-built. And all the other cabins are too far away. As for your lover, he's safely tucked away in his apartment and won't hear a thing."

Megan backed away. "What are you going to do?"

"Give you a ride in my speed boat. That isn't much to ask, is it?" Something glittered in his eyes, something that flashed her mind back to Jack.

"I told you not to go off to that church service."

"But Jack, you weren't even here. You didn't need me and I thought...."

"Don't think, just obey. Isn't that what your church teaches, to obey your husband?"

"Yes, but...."

"But nothing."

"Jack?" Her mind spun with confusion. What happened to the charming young man who swept her off her feet? This isn't what she left her parents for. "I try to obey you, but marriage is also about respect and love."

"Then you better respect my wishes." He staggered and would have fallen if she hadn't caught him. His breath gagged her.

"You've been drinking again."

She didn't even see his hand before it connected against her face.

Megan never forgot that look. It still had the power to turn her stomach into a mass of quivering panic. She saw that look in Bryce's eyes now.

"I don't want to go with you."

"You're going. Do you want to go as you are or would you prefer something more appropriate for a pleasant day's outing?"

"You'll stay out here."

He settled on the sofa. "As long as you hurry. The sun is rising, and I won't have anyone gawking at us."

Megan wondered how long she could stall. He sensed her thoughts. "If you take too long, I'll come dress you myself."

His threat set wings to her feet. Hurrying back into the bedroom, she threw her nightgown onto the unmade bed, pulled out jeans and a sweater and tugged them on. At the last minute, she pulled a hat down onto her head. In the bathroom, she washed up, took a painkiller...and prayed. Finally, she pulled on a thin jacket and buckled her cell into her pocket before tucking her hair into a cap.

She started when he knocked on the bedroom door. "It's time to go."

Fleetingly, she wished the lock on the door was stronger, but it would not stand against his weight. "Coming." As casually as possible, she opened the door.

"How about breakfast first?"

"I'm not a fool."

"All right. I have one more thing I need to do in the bedroom."

"Write a note? I think not."

He jerked her chin up and grinned into her face. Smelling liquor on his breath, she quailed. "Don't you know all your thoughts are mirrored on that face of yours?" He dropped her chin and took her arm. "Come on now." He escorted her to the door.

Glancing around, she prayed for someone, anyone, to show themselves, but she saw no one. The sky was clearing into day, and the birds trilled in the trees. A myriad of insects buzzed in the background. How could the day feel so normal when inside she felt only darkness?

Even so, as they stepped outside, she looked up toward Mark's condo. Before she opened her mouth, Bryce's hand clamped over it. Holding her in what must have appeared a lover's embrace, he walked her down the road, past the lodge, to the dock.

Cautiously releasing her, he motioned toward the sleek black cruiser bumping gently against the dock. "Beautiful, isn't she." It was not a question.

He pushed her forward. "Get in."

When she hesitated, he picked her up and threw her into the boat. She landed in a heap, gasping with pain as she landed on her bad leg. Did she see a shadow pass a window of the lodge?

"Help," she screamed. "Help me." The wind whipped the words from her mouth and flung them back into the lake.

Grinning, Bryce untied the boat and leaped aboard. "I told you it would do no good. Not out here. No one is going to hear you out here."

Rubbing her leg, she found her seat as far away from Bryce at the controls as she could. He laughed at her choice, knowing as she did, that wherever she sat, once on the lake, she was in his control. Recklessly, she grabbed the railing, but he hauled her back. Still holding her, he started the motor and zoomed away from the dock, once more knocking her to the floor.

On the other side of the bay, he cut off an early fisherman reaching out over the side. He toppled into the lake with a splash. Horrified, Megan turned back. Thankfully, the fisherman bobbed up again. Glancing back, she saw Bryce pull out a bottle and take a long swig.

"Want some?"

She shook her head. "You shouldn't drink and drive." Instinctively, she hurled her warning into the wind.

He only laughed and took another swig. Her hands gripped the railing until the knuckles whitened. Fear washed up into confusion like the white waves that splashed up around the hull, rocking the boat front to back, side to side.

"Where are we going?"

"You'll see." His teeth glinted in the newly risen sun.

"Lord Jesus, help me. Please keep me safe. Get us home safely." Bryce's driving worried her, but she tried not to think about it.

A gull, all white and gray, landed lightly on the water, then hurriedly took flight as Bryce deliberately steered the boat at the bird. Further away, a solitary loon cried, its mournful cry echoing her fears.

As he skirted the bay and headed out into the main lake, her hope for rescue diminished. Houses and trees and cabins and docks blurred as they roared by. Her light-weight jacket alternately hugged her body, then whipped away, as Bryce directed the boat this way and that. Megan ducked her head to keep the wind from scraping the cap from her head.

Another speedboat zoomed by, rocking them. She waved and tried to call, but the wind crammed her cries back down into her throat. Bryce laughed and waved back.

He continued to nurse his bottle, and his driving continued to get wilder and more erratic, but the speed did not lessen. Holding on, Megan surveyed the boat for a life preserver, but saw none. Not that she would have been able to put it on at this speed. Her leg ached abominably, and she wasn't sure it would even hold her weight.

She cried, "Slow down."

He shook his head. His laugh sent chills down her back and brought memories flooding back.

"You must stop drinking, Jack."

"Says who."

"Me. You're killing yourself and our marriage. I love you and want what is best for you, for us."

"You want to run my life, you mean. I don't need you preaching at me all the time, Megan."

"I'm only telling you this for your own good."

"Stop, please. If you would only consent to come along sometimes, you might find you enjoy my parties."

"I went, remember?"

"Once." His lip curled in derision. "You were such an embarrassment. On second thought, maybe you should stay home."

"Once was enough. I don't need to drink or do drugs to have a good time. And neither do you. What about us?"

"What about us?" Jack sniggered. "Come on. Go with me tonight."

"No."

"You must. I say so." He dragged her out to the car.

In her nightmares, she still heard the roar of the engine, his drunken laugh. On a steep curb, he lost control. *She* heard a scream. It was her own.

Absently, she rubbed her leg. Megan saw that same sullen, liquor-dazed look on Bryce's face. Panic licked inside. "Lord, how can I stop him? How?"

As she feared the worst, he pulled back on the controls. The boat slowed to a crawl. The white splash of the waves settled into a gentle lapping. Loons cried. Far away in another inlet, two riders raced each other on jet skies.

Totally ignoring her, Bryce stared out over the lake. Her hopes rose that he might listen to reason and take them back--slowly.

"Bryce."

"Yes, what is it?" He didn't look at her.

"You have a nice boat."

"I do, don't I." Turning his head, he grinned boyishly. "Bet I scared you some though, didn't I?"

"You did that," she agreed. "But this is nice. Sitting here, letting the sun beat down. It's going to be a warm day."

"Perfect weather to be out on the lake."

"Yes," she said with a smile, "but you could have been more polite about the invitation."

A shadow past over his face that gave her pause. "You wouldn't come."

"I'm here now. Thunder Lake is a beautiful lake."

"Beautiful setting for a beautiful lady."

She didn't like this turn in the conversation. "Thank you, Bryce. We've been out now for sometime. Maybe we should start back before someone gets worried."

"Your lover? He'll think you're just sleeping late."

"Mark is my friend, not my lover. I think you know that Bryce."

"But you prefer him to me."

Lord, how do I answer that one? She said nothing.

His face twisted, and, for a moment, she thought he would cry. She'd seen the maudlin stage, too, and the remorse, often short lived, that it brought.

The mirror showed an eye she wouldn't be able to take into public for days. Jack saw it too, and his face crumpled. Gentle as a breeze, he touched it.

"I'm sorry Meg. I didn't mean to hurt you. It's the drink."

"Then don't drink."

"I'll try."

She thought he did try, but it never lasted for long. He enjoyed the partying, the company, the bars, too much. She suspected more, but Megan thought as long as she didn't know for sure, it would be all right. Jack did try to change, and, for a week or so, things would be almost good.

For a short period of time, Jack listened. Megan planned to use that experience as an opportunity to change Bryce's mind and get him to start back.

"Bryce, let's go back. I've seen your boat. Others have seen you out here with me. We've had a nice ride. Let's go back."

"You're right of course," he said thoughtfully, then dashed her hopes. "Others have seen us together. What's in that? Nothing wrong with a young man giving his lady fair a turn about the lake, is there?"

"No, there's isn't," she said. "So now?"

"Don't nag."

"It was a question," she said evenly, her hands once more tightening on the rail.

"I'm tired of being nagged. Mother nags, you know. They think I'm spoiled, so she nags at me. Do you know why?"

"I can well imagine."

"My drinking," Tossing the bottle into the lake without a thought, he rummaged for another. Opening it, he took another long swallow. "Oh, she nags me about that enough. But they drink, too. Or didn't you know." Seeing her expression, he laughed.

"You really think everyone in the family is a saint? Well, they may claim to be saints, but they aren't nearly so uptight as the others. "

"Which means what?" Maybe he needed an audience.

"Means they take a nip or two. Took my first drink from their own bar. Dad grounded me for two whole days."

"I hate to see you like this, Bryce. You can be so nice when you aren't drinking. Why not set a course for home?"

His face tightened. "You'd like that wouldn't you? I'm not ready to leave yet. I got you out here to get you away from the leech who's turned your head."

"Mark?"

"You've never given me a fair chance."

"No, Bryce. I admit to be drawn to you at times, but you, not Mark, blew your own chances. I don't care to be assaulted."

He stared into the sky. "What would you say if I told you my attentions were serious?"

"Surprised. Are they?"

"Could be, with some encouragement."

"I've heard that line before, Bryce. It doesn't wash.

Besides, I don't feel that way about you. Not now."

"Because of Adrian."

Megan decided honesty was the only way. "Because of Mark."

"Has he proposed?"

"No. I don't know that he will." From the look on Bryce's face, she knew that last was a mistake.

"My parents like you. Did you know that? A nice, sensible, Christian girl." His gaze narrowed. "I hear them talking about you. How nice it would be if I would find someone like you. So I thought, why not you."

"I told you. No. We wouldn't get along. We're very different you and I."

"Because you're a Christian."

"That's part of it. Jesus does make a difference. Bryce, I cannot believe you are really happy with your life, at least not the morning after."

"What do you know about my life?"

Biting her lip, she turned away. "I married someone much like you. He could be so charming when he wanted to be. Other times, especially when he drank, he could be cruel."

Megan heard only silence behind her. The wind that had died down for a time started rising again, and her hair whipped her cheeks. She heard Bryce gun the motor, and the boat once more picked up speed.

"We're headed back. Thank you, Lord." Again the scenery whizzed passed. As he had done before, Bryce cut into a small inlet. A single fishing boat clunk, clunked against the dock.

Again he cut the motor, letting it idle just in the protection of the small cove. She could hear the trees whisper. A gull flew overhead, settled onto the water, and flew off again.

"So you think I'm just like your husband." Bryce's voice sounded so close, she jumped.

He sat next to her. She swung about. "Bryce. Not again. This has been done."

"Ah," he said with a decided grin, "but this time Adrian won't interfere."

Almost casually he draped an arm about her shoulders. "I want you, Megan. You should be more appreciative of that. It's not as though I want for female companions."

"But not those you can bring home."

"Maybe not, but they're fun nonetheless."

"Then stick with them and leave me alone."

"You don't understand do you? My dear mother, and father I might add, think it's time I carry on the family name, and soon. Dad has built up quite the business, and I inherit every last dime."

"Goodie for you," she said. "But money won't buy you happiness, Bryce. It never does."

"Wouldn't you like to wear diamonds around that pretty neck?" His fingers on her neck seemed vaguely threatening, and she pulled away.

"No, diamonds are not as important as knowing I am in God's will. He is the only true source of wealth and happiness." Strange, confrontations with Jack always left her humiliated, weak. A calm pervaded. Even though panic licked inside at what he might do to her, she also felt a deep concern for his welfare.

"Stop it," he ordered, and his expression chilled her. "I am tired of being nagged. I am tired of being preached at. And, I am tired of playing games with you, Meggie. I want you. Marry me."

Meggie? Jack called her that sometimes, and the name had less than happy associations. "Don't call me that. No, Bryce, I will not marry you. No."

He crushed her to his side. She twisted away. He grabbed. She ducked. Grabbing her shoulders, he shook her until her head rattled. Fury burst and she slapped him.

Stunned, he released her. She tried to reach the controls. If only she could gun the motor, it would give him something to think about other than her. Her leg slowed her down, and he pulled her back onto his lap. When she struggled, abuse poured from his mouth.

"Bryce. Stop. Stop it. Let me go."

He lowered his mouth to hers, but she turned her head and his kiss fell on her cheek. Roughly, he turned her head back and held it. Her stomach churned. Immobilized, she had no choice but to submit.

"I will not have some prude cramping my style," he growled. "You will be mine. One way or another, Megan, you will be mine."

"You're crazy," she shouted. "This is not the middle ages, and you're certainly not a knight in shining armor. I won't give in to this kind of threat. I won't!" Her mind flashed back.

"Where have you been Jack? I've been worried something happened to you. You've been gone three days. I almost called the police."

"You better not. My life is my life, and I won't have you or anyone else cramping her style."

"But I thought you were hurt."

"Would you care? Huh, dar...ling, Meggie?" His finger scraped her jaw, still sore from their last conflict. She didn't answer fast enough.

"See, you don't care anymore. But I do," He clamped her to him. His lips bruised hers until she struggled to get away. There was no escape.

There was none now. Megan fought Bryce, fought him with her draining strength and resources and heard him laugh. His hands began to roam her body. She screamed. There was no one to hear her.

"Jesus save me! Save me!" she screamed. "Jesus?"

Bryce released her so quickly, she slumped onto the floor. Pain knifed through her back.

"Stop it. Stop screaming." His gaze shot arrows of hate.

"Jesus," she whispered, recoiling from the frightening madman hovering over her. "Jesus."

"Take me back, Bryce."

He hauled her to her feet. For a moment, she thought he was going to listen. Instead, he grabbed for her again. With all her might, she pushed him away. He stumbled and fell against the controls, pushing the lever forward. The boat lunged ahead, flinging her against the railing. Her body arched over the foaming, churning water. Bryce grabbed the controls, whirling the boat around.

Her hold on the railing slipped. "Bryce," she screamed. "Help!"

It happened in an instant. Bryce turned. She lost her grip. He grabbed for her, but succeeded in knocking her off her precarious hold. She felt her body going over the side, flipping in the air. Her head struck something, she don't know what.

Megan heard Bryce yell her name, and again. She heard nothing more, except a distant roar of a speedboat that grew fainter and fainter and fainter.

CHAPTER THIRTEEN

*There is no fear in love; but perfect love casteth
out fear: because fear hath torment. He that feareth is not
made perfect in love.* I John 4:18

Water slapped Megan's face, stinging her awake.
Jerking, she gulped and spit out icy water. Around her,
water rose and fell as the wind blew over it. With each
swell, she bobbed up. As another wave washed over her,
she swallowed water and sank.

Clawing her way to the surface, she flailed her
arms in the water. Her water-soaked clothing dragged her
down, down. "No!"

Again she jerked up her head. The movement sent
a zillion pain sensors jangling in her head. Gingerly, she
touched her forehead. Her fingers came away sticky with
her own blood.

"Bryce." she called. "Bryce!"

The wood echoed and re-echoed her scream.
Silence. Deadly silence. No Bryce. No boat. She was
alone. The thought chilled her more than the lake water.

Desperately, she surveyed her position. Too far

from shore. Too far to drift in with the waves. Her leg throbbed in time to the agony in her head. It had been years since she had been swimming, and she'd never been very accomplished.

Pursing her lips, she sighted the shore. Forcing herself to relax, she let herself float. Tired, she needed to rest a moment before striking out. Megan didn't recall the inlet being so far away. After going overboard, she must have blacked out and drifted a ways before coming to. Her hands clutched a hefty branch that had probably kept her afloat.

"Lord, thank you for this branch," she called out, sputtering as she swallowed water. For a time, she floated on her back to retain strength. The sun warming her face accentuated the chill in her body.

"Lord," she prayed. "Help me. I don't know what happened to Bryce. I don't think he intended to harm me, at least not like this, but, Jesus, he left me. He left me to die, and I don't know if I can make it to the shore."

Inside she heard. *Swim. Swim.*

Sucking in a deep breath, she struck out for the shore in long slow strokes. Her injured leg hung almost limp and ached when she tried to force it to move. After trial and error, she compensated somewhat with the other leg, but it was slow going and difficult to keep a straight course.

Further, she tired easily and often stopped to rest, treading water so as not to float back into the main lake. If only more people were out on the lake today. "Lord, I could use someone to come by, say in a sailboat."

Deadly silence met her ears. She heard no engine humming, no distant laughter, only loons crying and gulls splashing on the water. An insect buzzed by her head and another. Shaking them off, she ducked under the water and tried to swim away from them. She came up gasping for air, her stomach churning and sloshing from water she must have taken in when she went overboard.

"Jesus," she gasped out, time and again, but there was little energy to pray. "Take care of me."

Trust me.

"I do. I do."

Even as she struggled toward the shore that seemed to only inches closer, a peace enveloped her. Whatever happened, she knew. She knew without a shadow of doubt that God was in control and that she could trust him with her life.

With the peace came a new understanding. She no longer needed to try to seek God's favor. She'd heard that before, but now she lived it, and the revelation freed her from chains of the past. He would take care of her in life...and death.

So clearly did she see him that tears mingled with the lake water. For the first time in her life she had no fear of a God of judgment. Jesus Christ was a God of love and he loved her, just as she was. Megan West belonged to him. She could die with that comfort. And, Megan was convinced her life was going to end right here, struggling against the rising waves.

Safety? She'd already found it in Christ. Her thoughts turned to Mark and her heart cried. How would he hear the news? Would he believe she went with Bryce willingly? She stopped. Would anyone even know what happened to her? She doubted Bryce would confess.

And dear Michael. How would he deal with losing someone else he loved? Would he think she deserted him? Would Mark?

"No! I will not give up. I can't!" This time, peace gave her strength, and, once more, she struck out toward shore. Megan battled herself as much as the water. Her breath started between her clenched teeth, and her arms shook with exhaustion.

Just as she felt herself slip under the surface, the water warmed; the waves eased. Surrounded by the protective trees, the tiny inlet stretched out before her. The gentle waves rippled languidly toward shore. Exhausted, she lay back and let herself be carried in.

As her toes touched bottom, she began paddling again until she felt sand against her chest. Her lungs bursting, she pulled herself up on the beach and collapsed.

How long she slept, she had no idea, but already the sun had reached its zenith. The sun had not only dried, but scorched the exposed parts of her body. Somewhere she'd lost her cap, so nothing protected her face. Her cheeks burned, and her hands felt like claws. Nevertheless, it felt good to be at least somewhat dry.

A large black Labrador licked her burning cheeks, barked when she groaned and raised her head. His tongue on her burn felt like sandpaper. Again he barked and ran up the incline into the woods.

Heaving herself to her feet, she stared after him, discerning a narrow path through the trees. A path might lead to a road or a cabin. Shakily, she stood up and tested her leg. Her head spun dizzily. Her leg buckled under her, and she fell headlong onto the beach. Yuck! She came up spitting out warm sand.

This time she sat up more slowly and waited for her head to clear. Touching her forehead, she found blood congealed around the wound. Crawling forward into the shadow of the trees, she leaned against the trunk of a tall pine to catch her breath. She felt a bump against her side. Her cell! The buttoned pocket held it secure. She pulled it out and shook out water. Ugh! At the very least it would need to be dried out before she attempted to use it. With a grimace, she stuck it back into the pocket.

With a sigh, she glanced around at her immediate surroundings for a stout branch about the height of a cane. Stretching, she grabbed a good possibility and snapped off the small branches. Using her good leg, she levered herself up the trunk of the tree, letting it support her while she tested the strength of the thick branch.

Cautiously, she shifted her weight to the branch. It held. "Thanks, Lord," she whispered.

Megan hobbled down the path taken by the dog. Once she tripped on a root, another time the dizziness in her head grew so great she had to rest. As soon as it passed, she continued on.

The Lab returned, barking and zipping around her until she feared he'd knock her over. "Go home," she commanded as sternly as she could manage.

From large eyes, he looked at her, before dashing into a clearing ahead. She found him sitting on the doorstep of a rustic cabin. Though the place appeared deserted, the presence of the obviously well-cared-for animal told her either the cabin was inhabited or the dog was as lost as she. It was still a cabin.

Relief washed over her, making her so weak, she found it difficult to manage the last few steps to the door. She knocked. No one answered. She knocked louder. No answer. She yelled. Nothing. Megan knocked and yelled. The dog stared at her.

Glancing around, she saw no vehicles. Great! Tears of disappointment stung her eyes.

"Lord, I got all this way for nothing."

On a strong impulse, she tried the door knob. It turned beneath her hand. The door swung open with a minute squeak. The dog whizzed past her into the small interior. She followed his bark into the tiny kitchen.

He waited for her, and she could not help but pet and encourage him as she surveyed the room. A small table was jammed into the corner between an oven and a refrigerator. Above the table a small window framed the trees outside. Next to the stove, a sink held several unwashed plates. A door opened into a combination living-sleeping area. Beside the door, a phone.

Call Mark. She had to call Mark. Weakly she

leaned against the door frame to steady herself. Concentrating, she recalled his mobile phone number and dialed. The phone rang and rang and rang, and she prayed he had his phone with him.

"Please answer. Please Lord, let him hear it."

On the tenth ring, a masculine voice came on line. "Hello."

"Oh, Mark," she managed, and began to cry.

"Megan Honey, where are you? Are you all right?"

The warmth of his voice swept away the vestiges of control. "Mark, help me. Please."

His alarm vibrated through the line. "Megan, where are you? What happened?" And again, "Are you all right?"

"I don't know."

"Don't know where you are or if you're all right?"

"Both." Trying to stem the tears, she choked into the phone. "Come get me," she asked like a little child. "Please come get me."

"Honey. You have to tell me where you are. I've been worried about you. We all have. Michael's frantic, and even Bryce is searching the woods with the others."

"Bryce. Oh, Mark. Bryce knows where I am. He...he..." The words stuck in her throat as the horror of what he had done swept over her. "He left me to die, Mark."

"What!" Fury exploded the line. "That no good...."

She sensed he calmed himself with effort. "Can you describe your location?"

"I am in some small inlet. There was one battered fishing boat tied up at the dock. I...I'm calling from a small cabin up from the beach in the woods. You can't see it from the lake." Rubbing her head, which pounded like a ten ton truck over rails, she tried to think. "There's a nice black Lab, a dog. No one is home."

"Can you read the number on the phone?"

Hope rose and sank. "It is too faded."

"At least you are relatively safe for the moment, aren't you?"

"Y...e...s." She knew she had to sit down or fall.

Mark heard her hesitation. "Megan honey, you are all right?"

"I hit my head when I fell, and it hurts. Everything spins around. And my leg. It doesn't want to hold up. Mark, I have to sit down. Please find me."

"MEGAN!"

Megan scarcely managed to hang up the phone before she blacked out. She awoke with the dog over her, gently nudging her. He whined his concern. Reaching up, she patted his sleek head. "Thanks fellow. Your owner must be a nice person to have a dog like you."

Reacting to her tone, the dog wagged his tail and licked her cheek. His tongue ignited a thousand burned cells, and she pushed him away. "Not now, fellow."

Afternoon rays cast long shadows across the dim interior of the room. For a moment, she blinked her eyes to adjust them. "Lord Jesus, it's getting dark. Please let Mark find me--somehow."

She tried to think, but her mind refused to cooperate. Instead, she focused on getting to her feet and finding a more comfortable place to wait. Blood had begun to seep from her head wound. She wiped it away with the sleeve of her jacket.

It was getting late in the day. Maybe the owner of the cabin would return and take her back to Five Geese Flying Lodge.

Cautiously, she felt for her branch cane only to find it in two pieces. It must have snapped when she fell. She crawled, wincing with each move, to the only chair in the kitchen, a tall ladderback, which she managed to pull out before heaving herself onto the seat. Bowing over the table, she breathed in deeply until her heart rate lessened.

Again the dog whined, his head on her lap. She patted his head while considering her position. Mark was correct, for the moment she was safe. She was also hungry for she hadn't eaten since last night.

Eyeing the refrigerator, she scooted the chair to the left, enough for her to reach the handle. The ancient refrigerator, yellow with age, resisted her first attempt. Gritting her teeth, she jerked. It popped open so quickly, she fell back against the back of the chair.

Gazing from her to the refrigerator and back, the dog tilted his head in perfectly clear verbal clues. "You hungry, too? Well, let's see what we have." She talked out loud, and the dog seemed to understand.

Unfortunately, getting at the food was more difficult than opening the door. With a sigh, she pushed herself to her feet. Resting most of her weight on the table, she drew out a pint of milk (half empty), an opened packaged of sliced white cheese and half a loaf of whole wheat bread. After shutting the refrigerator, she sat down again.

Megan opened the bread sack and tossed the dog a slice, which he ate in one gulp, and looked for more. She gave him another with a firm, "That's it. I don't know whether or not your owner permits you to eat people food."

The dog sat, his tail thumping the floor. His soft pleading gaze undermined her determination, and she soaked another piece of bread with milk and fed it to him. With that he lay down, still watching her, but evidently satisfied.

She slapped three slices of Swiss cheese on one piece of bread and topped them with another. She looked around for glasses and plates, but found nothing she could reach, at least, not without expending more energy than she had left. Shrugging, she ate her sandwich, and, with only slight hesitation, drank the milk straight from the carton.

Megan finished off the milk. Leaning back, she sighed with the contentment of satisfaction. The meal served to strengthen her. It did more. It also sharpened her mind.

For the moment, the pain receded in her head. Her leg, too, felt better. "Thank you, Lord. Thank you."

Once more, she levered herself to her feet to return

the bread and cheese to the refrigerator. She sat back down with a plop. Laying her head on the table, she tried to pray and plan. What would she do if the owner did not return soon or if Mark couldn't find her? How could he? Her information had been less than helpful.

I know where you are.

"I know Lord."

Do you trust me to take care of you?

She hesitated but a moment. "Yes, Lord. I know you will take care of me no matter what."

The verses from Matthew came to mind, *"Come unto me, ... and I will give you rest."*

It felt so good to rest. Surely she could rest a while. She was safe. Jesus was with her.

***

"Megan. Megan honey. Oh, Lord." Was it, the prayer rumbling deep in Mark's throat or the growl of the dog that pierced her sleep?

Groggily, she lifted her head and stared at Mark kneeling beside her, his face twisted with anger and concern. "Megan?"

"Mark," she choked out. "You found me." The dog tried to wedge himself between them. Grinning foolishly, she patted his head. "Friend," she told him. "Friend." He sat back, watching.

Mark's arms enfolded her. "You're knight is here, Honey,"

Megan snuggled in his embracing arms as he whispered, "Praise the Lord, we found you."

She pushed away. "We?" she glanced past him to find Bryce hulking in the shadows, a strange look on his face, his hands in the pockets of his slacks. The last rays of the sun shooting through the window lit up the left side of his face that had swelled into a repulsive greenish-purple. She glanced at Mark's bruised knuckles. The dog growled.

"Bryce." She could not help the rise in her voice. "You brought him here?"

"Shh." Mark pushed her lank hair from her cheeks damp with relieved tears. She felt a rumble deep in his chest. "With some persuasion, he agreed to show me where you, ah, fell overboard." His eyes flashed at Bryce and back at her.

"That's a nasty bump," he said, carefully inspecting her face. Setting her firmly back in the chair, he went to the sink. Rummaging in the cupboard, he found paper towels, wet them and gently wiped her face.

"I'm sure I look dreadful."

He laughed then. "Umm. You can't be that bad off if you're worried about your appearance."

"Bryce," he ordered, "hand her that first aid kit we brought along."

Taking it, Mark snapped it opened, took out two large pads and tape that he used to bind up her head after applying an antiseptic. "There, feel better?" She nodded, careful not to move too quickly.

"Now didn't you say something about your leg?"

Biting her lip, she nodded again. "How did you get up here? It's quite a climb."

"I found a branch to lean on." She motioned to the floor. "It snapped when I fell."

"Think you can stand now."

"I don't know."

Bryce stepped forward. Megan flinched, her arms automatically reaching for Mark. He enfolded her. "Listen, Megan. I didn't mean to hurt you. I didn't. I thought...I thought you were.... It was the drink, you understand." He had never seemed so unsure of himself. She turned away.

Mark growled, "You left her to die."

"I thought she was dead. That's what scared me. Megan, I...."

No one noticed the door open until a middle aged man with a decided paunch and thinning hair, growled, "What's going on here? Why did you break into my cabin?"

The dog leaped to his feet, his tail wagging.

Mark straightened. "Who are you?"

"I could ask you the same. I'm Grant McKerne, and this is my cabin."

Mark nodded. "Nice to meet you. I am Mark Adrian and this is Megan West. We're staying at Five Geese Flying Lodge." He ignored Bryce who lingered in the shadows.

In a few terse words, Mark summed up the situation. "I see. Does she need medical attention? Can I drive you back?"

"The boat's faster," Mark said, thanking the man. "Her cousin Peter is a doctor. We'll have him look at her."

"Wait. I must pay for the food I ate." Megan glanced at the man. "I'm afraid I shared some with your dog."

Grant laughed and patted the animal's head. "I know how he can beg. But no need to reimburse me. I'm just glad the cabin, and Midnight, were here to help."

Mark shoved some cash into his hands. "Buy Midnight something special."

Picking Megan up in his strong arms, Mark headed for the door. Mr. McKerne watched them go, the dog at his side.

"Thank you," she called back to him. "You have a very special dog."

Bryce lumbered along behind. Shutting her eyes, she cushioned her head against Mark's solid shoulder. She didn't want to think of Bryce. Or Jack.

Around them, the trees whispered their secrets. The wind, which had been so strong earlier, softened to a gentle breeze. Midnight followed them down to the dock and watched as Mark carefully handed her into Bryce's boat. She shuddered at the sight of it, but Mark was immediately beside her, wrapping her in a blanket, and, blessedly, his arms.

Without a word, Bryce moved to the driver's seat and started the motor. "I don't trust him," she murmured.

Bryce's face whitened, and she could see his hands shake. "I'll get you home safely Megan. I promise you that." Something in his voice assured her he would do just that.

The motor roared into life, and Mark's arms tightened as the boat leaped forward. Bryce held a steady course from the bay back to the resort. "You really must stop hitting your head," Mark whispered, his breath warm on her cheek.

As he hoped, she relaxed.

When they arrived, Jay met them at the dock. "You found her. Good." He held the boat to the dock, allowing Mark to scoop Megan up and leap safely over.

"Do you know where her cousin Peter is?"

"Think they all went down to the tent when I gave the signal that they could stop searching. I'll get him." He motioned to the cart parked nearby. "Use that to take her back."

"Thanks." Carefully settling her on the comfortable seat, Mark took over the controls. The little cart jerked once before starting forward. The motion set her head to spinning again, but when she breathed deeply it eased.

Mark stopped directly in front of her door. By the time he had carried her in and laid her on the couch, Peter was framed in the doorway.

"Cousin, I am supposed to be on vacation. What's this, another hit on the head?" Though his words teased, she saw the darkness in his eyes. "I understand Bryce had something to do with this."

"Both times," Mark growled. "She hurt her leg as well as her head this time."

"Megan. Oh, Megan," Selma asked, entering the condo, "how are you doing? Peter?"

"I haven't had time to examine her, Selma."

She pursed her lips. "That boy. He's been trouble since he was a baby. I warned them to discipline, but no, nothing was too good for the lad. Look where it got him."

Putting his hands on her shoulders, Peter firmly moved her aside. "Selma, I need to examine her. Good thing I always bring an emergency bag, just in case."

Pulling up a chair, he asked questions as he probed the wound in her head. "Does this hurt? This? Do you know how long you were out? Were you dizzy? Are you now? Here let me put some salve on that face and neck."

His exam continued. When he finished bandaging her head, he advised, "Rest. No boating, nothing strenuous. Wouldn't hurt to get an x-ray just in case."

"Don't worry, Doc. I'm not exactly up to running a marathon at the moment."

"Her leg, Peter," Mark reminded.

"Yes, I should look at that." A muscle in his cheek twitched. "Sorry cousin, but for me to get a proper look, the jeans have to come off."

Megan blushed. "Are you sure? All right, but not here."

Mark said, "I'll take her to the bedroom," Suiting words to action, he picked her up and carried her to the bedroom where he set her down on the edge of the bed.

"I'm going to find Michael to let him know you're in reasonably fair shape. Then I'll be back."

"Mark." she touched his arm. "Thanks."

Leaning down, he gently kissed her lips. "We'll talk later."

After he left, Aunt Selma came in and helped her out of her clothing and into a robe. Selma found her cell. "Wet. Umm. I'll see what Mark can do with it. All right?" Selma, absently stuck into a wide pocket.

Megan nodded, but hardly cared.

"She's ready," Selma called from the door.

"You'll stay, won't you Aunt Selma."

"Fine thing," he growled. "Not trusting your doctor."

She blushed. "I...."

He brushed away her embarrassment. "Don't worry about it, Megan. These days it's always safer for a doctor to have a witness."

She flared, "If you think I'd sue or anything."

"That a girl," he chuckled. "That perked you up. Now lean back, and let me check that leg."

Reluctantly, she exposed her scar. He didn't flinch, but she heard Aunt Selma's quickly stifled gasp. "What happened?" Peter asked.

"My husband was drunk and smashed up the car."

"And it left your hip weak."

"Yes." Gently, he probed her leg while he asked questions. "If we were at my office, I'd order x-rays, but..."

"Is it serious, Peter? I won't lose the use of my leg, will I?"

"No, nothing like that. From what I can tell, your leg got wrenched, and, since it was already weak, it collapsed. Stay off of it as much as possible for a couple of days, and I think you'll be almost back to normal. I do recommend you have your doctor check you over more thoroughly once you get home. Actually, if we can find a local doctor, I'd see about getting both your head and leg x-rayed tomorrow."

"We'll see, doctor," she said, then groaned as pain zipped down her leg. "Meanwhile how am I going to get around?"

"Can you walk at all?"

"I don't know." With his assistance, she stood up and took a couple of steps. Without his steadying arm, she would have collapsed from the pain.

Setting her back on the bed, he said thoughtfully. "You need some kind of crutch. I'll find something that will do until tomorrow. By then, we can hopefully find something in town. But first take this." He pulled out several small foil packages. "I travel with lots of samples." He nodded to her OTC pain killers. "These will help more than those."

Selma brought a glass of water, and Peter waited until she'd taken a pill. "That should make you feel much better. I'll leave several of these. Take them every four hours as needed." He closed his case. "Now for the crutch."

Her aunt frowned. "Where are you going to find a crutch?"

Peter grinned. "I once took a mission trip to Nigeria. I discovered one can make due with supplies on hand. I'll see ya. Meanwhile, Cousin, maybe with Selma's able assistance, you could clean up a bit."

Megan threw a pillow at him. He ducked out just in time. "I'll be back when you're more presentable."

She was exhausted. She also felt dirty. Her hair hung limply around her face. "I need a shower, but my head."

"Phooey. If I can't re-bandage you, we'll make Peter do it when he returns. Come on." With Selma's help, she hobbled to the bathroom. By propping herself against the wall, she was able to manage a shower. How good it felt. The stinging hot water eased away assorted aches and pains. Unfortunately, she could view numerous other bruises down her arms and legs.

The hot water stung her face and cheeks, but she didn't care. Megan scrubbed her hair until it stopped smelling of lake water and sand.

She'd just gotten into a soft, comfortable burgundy jogging suit when Peter returned, triumphantly holding a sturdy wooden crutch made out of a stout board and crosspiece. "Jay had this lying around, and Rose told me to go ahead and use it."

It worked perfectly. With it under her arm, she hobbled into the living room just as Mark exploded through the door.

"Megan. Michael's missing, and no one knows where he is."

Peter frowned. "He was with me in the woods. I didn't want him to get lost. He did return with me. After Jay came for me, I thought I saw him down at the dock."

Mark's shoulders relaxed. "Then he has to be around somewhere."

"I don't know, Mark," Peter licked his lips. "The boy was down at the dock when I came up. Bryce was there, too, in his boat. I didn't think anything about it then, but now...."

Megan's stomach churned. Mark went white. "He wouldn't, Bryce wouldn't take revenge out on Michael. Not Michael!"

CHAPTER FOURTEEN

Hear me when I call, O God of my righteousness: thou hast enlarged me when I was in distress; have mercy upon me, and hear my prayer. Psalm 4:1

"Surely not." Mark reached for Megan, pulling her close, she thought, as much to comfort himself as her. "We have to find Bryce."

"Maybe he's down at the tent with the others," Peter suggested, "if he's still around. We shouldn't jump to conclusions."

Selma's hands dug into her hips. "Michael is such a dear boy," Selma said. "And a bright one. First, we need to make certain he isn't on the grounds, before making wild accusations." Megan bit her lip, anger flushing her cheeks as Selma defended Bryce. "I know it looks bad for Bryce, but...."

Mark's expression was dark with concern. "Well, I can't stand around here. I've got to look for Michael."

"Yes." Megan felt a check within. "But first we need to pray."

Mark's arms tightened around her. "Lord, help us find my son. Don't let anything happen to him. I...."

His voice broke, and she continued, "Lord, keep Michael safe. Help him not to be afraid, but to know you are with him."

Peter took over as she finished, "Lord, we bind the forces of evil and ask that you open our minds and hearts to know how to go about finding Michael."

Selma hesitated but a moment before adding, "Lord, whatever happens, I pray that you will lead Bryce to yourself. Take care of this dear little boy."

Anger flared at her aunt's petition. Megan felt less than generous toward the man who left her for dead and may well have kidnapped a young boy.

Again she sensed that check within, *You don't know that.*

She forced back the thought.

"I think," Peter said, "the way to go on this is to gather everyone down at the tent."

Selma nodded. "Most everyone is all ready there anyway, waiting to hear how you are, Megan."

"I'll let Rose and Jay know what's going on," Mark said. "They know the place almost as well as that son of mine."

"I want to help." Megan griped his arm. "What can I do?"

"Stay here." Mark's tone left no doubt of his thoughts. "I have enough to worry about right now, without adding you to the list."

Megan winced, unable to disguise her hurt. His expression softened. "Megan honey. I couldn't bear it, if you got hurt again."

When both Peter and Selma backed him up, she had little choice, but to agree. From the doorway, she watched as they headed down the slope to the tent. Mark detoured to the lodge.

"Bryce. Who would talk to Bryce?" Peter told her to sleep, but sleep was the last thing on her mind right now. Cautiously, she hobbled outside and sat down on the comfortable seat of the golf cart.

In the distance, she heard voices, but could make out only fragments carried on the breeze. It seemed years since Bryce forced her to leave with him, rather than the same day. So much had happened. All she could see was Bryce drinking more and more deeply and fear tying her up inside.

Shaking her head, slowly, so as not to start the buzzing in her head again, she marveled at her belief that the Christian life was an easy path. Since turning her life over to Christ, she had known nothing but trouble.

Admittedly, she also felt more alive than ever, and, even now, a certain peace calmed her. Something inside had changed. She savored the knowledge. Even Jack's image did not pain her so sharply.

Deliberately she remembered. There were good times. She recalled those. The roses for no reason, the singing telegram, the dinner theater tickets--all surprises. At first she blamed the change on his addiction to drink.

This time she knew the truth. Jack chose his way of life, and it did not include the Lord or, toward the end, her.

That hurt. She remembered that morning. He was finishing his packing when she entered the bedroom.

"Meggie, I didn't see you come in. I'm just about finished here. Now, where are those tickets." Picking them up from the dresser, he glanced in the mirror, his gaze focusing on her face that sported yet another black eye.

For a moment pain twisted his face, and remorse. "I'm sorry, you know."

"I know." She was tired of this replay. "The plane leaves in an hour."

"You're glad, aren't you?"

She merely shrugged. She had nothing more to offer.

He came toward her, and she flinched when he raised his hand. He winced at her response. Gently, he touched her cheek. "I am not the kind of man you deserve, Meggie. I hope someday you'll find someone who appreciates you properly." He kissed her cheek. "Good-bye Meggie. I wish you a good life."

"If you would stop drinking."

His eyes clouded. "I....I've been thinking on it, Meggie. I've been thinking on it. Maybe sometime."

"When you return home?"

He stepped back. "I know you don't believe this now, but I do care for you, Meggie. Not like you deserve, but I care."

The revelation hit and left her gasping. He never meant to come home. In his own way, he protected her. He knew how she felt about divorce, though it might well have come to that. She saw that, too. So he left to protect her from his abuse. Did he think she would eventually file?

Was his reckless lifestyle a death wish? An attempt to run from himself? Lowering her head, for the first time she allowed herself to grieve for Jack, for his misspent life, for what might have been. With the grieving came forgiveness and letting go.

Lifting her head, she watched as the Salstrand family fanned out on the grounds and on into the woods. Flashlights illuminated the shadows. She couldn't see Mark. Her heart quickened at the very thought of him.

"Lord, please take care of Michael. Please."

On the lake, the moonlight glinted off a boat slowly coming in to dock. Her breath started between her lips. She recognized that stance, the silver of the boat, the blue purpling under the flood light. Bryce.

So no one had talked to him. Feeling the wheel under her hand, she put the little cart in gear and pressed down the pedal. "Lord, help me."

After a couple of false starts, she managed to turn the wheel and head down to the road. Bryce's shoes clomped on the dock when she parked in front of him.

"Megan. What are you doing here?"

Under the lights, he looked pale. She wondered if she looked the same. His shoulders sagged. His glance slid by her to the dark forest beyond. "Why are you here? Where's your bodyguard?" His attempt at sarcasm failed, and he fell silent.

"He's out looking for his son Michael. So is everyone else. But he wants to talk to you."

Startled, he met her questioning gaze. "The boy's gone?"

"Yes. No one has seen him since Peter saw you talking to him after Mark brought her back."

Bryce stiffened. "What's this? Are you accusing me?"

"Well, you certainly have given cause to question your motives."

Raking his fingers through his hair, Bryce sucked in a deep breath. "I don't kidnap children."

"But you do leave a cousin to die," Mark growled as he marched onto the dock. Megan sensed the tight control he kept on his temper. "Megan, what are you doing here? I don't want you anywhere near this...this...."

"Look, I had nothing to do with the boy's disappearance."

"Megan," Mark put a hand on her shoulder. "Go back to your condo."

She met his gaze steadily. "I am part of this, Mark."

Tension tightened his face. "I know, but...."

"There you are Bryce." They turned to face Bryce's father. He looked old. "How could you, Son? First Megan, then a child?"

Bryce's expression hardened. "I did nothing with the child. He yelled something at me, but I wasn't about to listen. I headed out, and haven't been back since."

Mark moved forward. "I don't believe you."

"Son, you've been in trouble since you were thirteen. It will go easier for you if you tell the truth. Help us find the boy." Her heart went out to the high-profile businessman, humbled by his own son.

Something about the look on Bryce's face gave her pause. His eyes were clear, and on his cheeks she saw evidence of tears. She clutched Mark's shirt. "Mark, Dan. He may be telling the truth."

Mark swung about, and glared at her. "You defend him after what he did to you?"

"No, I do not excuse that, but I think he may be telling the truth about this." Turning to her cousin, she asked, "Have you been drinking?"

"No, not since," he could not meet her eyes until he finished, then his gaze held hers. "Not since I left you. I went out to get stinking drunk, instead all I could think of were the things you said to me." He shrugged. "Believe it or not, I poured all my stuff overboard. Probably have some pretty happy fish right now." His attempt at levity failed as his sarcasm had earlier.

Mark clenched and unclenched his fists. "So you say. I have to find Michael. If you don't know, who does?"

Megan touched his arm. "God knows, Mark? God is with him wherever he is."

Wistfully, Bryce said, "You truly believe that don't you? I wish I could believe, but I've done too much."

Mark stared at him then, hearing the same thing she did. This was no act. "If you didn't, then who?" He choked on the thought, "If he's out in the woods, a bear might find him before we do."

Bryce's father squeezed his shoulder. "Everyone who is able is out searching. If we don't find him soon we'll call in re-enforcements."

"This might not mean anything," Bryce said, "but...."

Mark coaxed, "Out with it man"

"Michael was not alone. Jonathan was with him. Has anyone talked to Jonathan?"

"Surely, if he knew anything, he would have spoken up," Bryce's father said. "You can do better than put the blame on another child."

Bryce turned away from his father. "You never did listen to me. You always were too busy to do more than bail me out of trouble. Don't you get it, Dad? I didn't care about your money until I realized it was the only thing *you* cared about. I needed you, not your money. I didn't matter; pretty soon I didn't care either."

He left his father gasping. "You aren't trying to blame your problems on me, are you? Not what you did to Megan here?"

It came out as a sneer. "No, I've made my own hellish choices." His voice sounded hollow in the once more rising wind.

"I suggest," Mark stepped in with his suggestion, "that we find Jonathan and talk to him. Bryce, you stay where we can see you. As for you," he addressed Megan, "can you get back to your place all right?"

"Yes, of course, but I want to know what's going on."

Leaning down, Mark grazed her cheek with a kiss. "You have the most difficult task--to pray."

Megan knew she must be content with that. As she headed back, she watched the trio make their way to the tent where Uncle Bob served as point man, keeping things organized. Even from the road, she heard the wind snap the edges of the tent. Her head had begun aching again and her eyes wanted to drift shut, but she forced herself to stay alert.

Turning down toward the condo, she jerked the cart to a stop as a shadow darted in front of her. "What? Who? Cassie what are you doing here?"

Reluctantly, the girl stopped. The yard light on the other side of the road cast light on cheeks wet with tears. "Cassie. What's wrong?"

"Oh, Megan...Miss West. They're looking for Jonathan."

"Yes, they want to ask him some questions."

"I...gotta go." Cassie started edging around the cart.

Catching her arm, Megan stopped her. "Come sit with me, Cassie, and tell me what's wrong."

The little blond plopped down on the seat next to her. "I can't. I can't tell. I promised."

Questions paraded through Megan's mind, and memories. She hid her bruise under make up before her folks came to visit. Dad must have suspected all was not well.

"How you doing, Honey?"

"F...fine Daddy. Just fine."

"Where's Jack? Is he going out to dinner with us?"

"He's busy, and will be late." Absently, she touched her sore face.

Dad looked skeptical. "You know we love you, Megan. That will never change, even though you went against our will to marry Jack. I'm still willing to listen to my girl."

"I'm all grown up now, Daddy."

Thoughtfully, he said, "Megan, things don't always go as we plan, but remember there is always someone willing to listen. Even when we're not near--God is. I firmly believe in being loyal to your vows, but there are times to ask for help. When that time comes, don't hesitate to call."

He left it at that. She never called. Then it was too late, and they were gone. Too long, she held the secret of her marriage, and it led to disaster. Like her father, she had to let Cassie know it was all right to reveal her secret. Megan had to know because she knew, somehow she knew, Cassie held a key to Michael's disappearance. *Lord, help her to handle this right? Guide her words.*

Settling back, she looked at the girl who wiped her

face with her jacket sleeve. "Cassie. Sometimes, if keeping a promise puts someone in danger, it's best to tell what you know. Michael is missing. Is your brother missing, too?"

Cassie bit her lip. "This is very important, Cassie. It is dark and the woods can be dangerous, especially at night."

"They're not in the woods, they're...." She turned away.

"They're where, Cassie? Where did Jonathan and Michael go?"

"I promised." Cassie stared out over the lake, and Megan's insides churned.

"Cassie, are they out on the lake?"

After giving her a long look, Cassie nodded. "I saw them go, and they made me promise not to tell. No one even knew Jon was gone."

"Because you pretended to know where he was."
Again she nodded.

"You know that was a lie."

"Y...yes." She sniffed. "But it got dark, and they didn't come back, and I got scared, and I didn't know what to do and are they all right and, and." She ran out of breath.

"Cassie I can't answer all your questions. Do you know why they left?"

She shook her head. "Michael wanted to go away. He'd been crying, but Jon wouldn't let him go alone. Said they'd be Tom Sawyer and Huck Finn."

"How did they go?"

"In a fishing boat. Jon knew how to run it. I think Michael did, too."

She had to know. "Did Bryce see them go?"

"Oh, no. There wasn't anyone around."

Oh, Lord. Where could they be? Please keep those boys safe. Putting an arm around the girl, she held her close for a moment. "Thank you Cassie. I'm sure glad you knew about this. It just might help us find them."

"They won't be mad at me?"

"Cassie, I think they'll be more than happy to be found." Pushing down on the pedal, Megan swung the cart around and sent it headlong down the road, around the lodge, down the beach to the tent.

"Mark. Mark! I know what happened to Michael," she called out as she drove the cart right into the tent.

Mark ran toward her. "Where is he? Did you know Jonathan is also missing?"

Bryce stood behind him. "I didn't do it?"

"I know." She looked at Mark. "They took off in a fishing boat. Cassie saw them go."

He stared out on the lake. "White caps. It's dangerous out there." His shoulders slumped. "How will we ever find them out there on a night like this?"

CHAPTER FIFTEEN

And we know that all things work together for good to them that love God, to them who are the called according to his purpose. Romans 8:28

In a long stride, Bryce stepped forward and grabbed Cassie. Shaking her back and forth, he demanded. "Where are those brats? I am not taking the fall for this, girl. Now, I want to know. Where they are?"

Mark jerked him back. "Keep your hands off her."

"I don't know. I don't know. I don't *know*!" Cassie bawled. "They got in a boat and went away. Michael didn't wanta stay. He was crying, too."

She wiped her nose on her sleeve. Putting an arm about her, Megan let her snuggle close. "Just tell us what you know. That's a girl. No one will hurt you."

"He won't touch me again?"

Mark glared at Bryce. "Not a chance." Stilling his own impatience, he knelt down beside Cassie and questioned her, but she knew little more than what she'd all ready told them.

Megan felt the disappointment reflected in Mark's

eyes. She asked, "Why would Michael leave?"

Mark's gaze lingered on her face. "I think I know." He turned to Uncle Bob and Dan. "Let's call the others back in and plan our new strategy. If this weather gets any worse...."

Uncle Bob shot a pistol in the air twice. Waited a moment and shot twice again. Within minutes, individuals hurried into the tent, all asking the same question. "Did you find him? Is he safe?"

Mark had to shout over the confusion. "No, but he is not in the woods. We do know that."

Mr. Hanson called out, "Where do we look now?"

"Daddy," Cassie cried, jumping from the cart and flinging herself against her father. "I'm sorry. I'm so sorry."

Puzzled, he lifted her into his arms. "Why aren't you asleep with your brothers and sister?"

"Oh, Daddy, I lied. Jonathan isn't 'sleep. He went away with Michael."

"What!" He stiffened. "Jonathan's gone? Why didn't you tell us sooner, Cassie?"

"I promised." She sniffed. "Jon made me promise. Mommy said I had to keep my promises."

"Yes. Yes, that's right," he told her absently, his face strained. "Where did they go, Cass?"

"Out on the lake."

"Oh, Lord." His prayer dropped out as a desperate plea. "Why?" His anguished gaze found Mark. "Why?"

His expression grim, Mark said, "We need to find

them first."

Uncle Bob straightened, his expression tight. "I agree."

The three teens joined the melee. It was the first time they looked less than perfectly turned out. Bits of twigs and leaves stuck in their hair, and exhaustion showed on their faces. Fleetingly, Megan wondered if her face was as pale as theirs in the lantern light.

Spotting them, their father motioned for them. "Girls will you take Cassie and see that she gets to bed. Stay with the kids and send Mrs. Hanson here." He paused. "Jonathan is also gone."

Once they left, Bryce spoke out. "I'm willing to go out. We can double up and each search part of the lake. I have a map and there are others. Right Jay?"

"I have several up at the lodge. A couple of the boats have GPS. If you can get a signal, use your phones."

Mark looked at Mr. Hanson. Mr. Hanson looked at Mark. "Let's do it."

"I'll get the maps," Rose said, "and meet you down by the dock."

As the others began to move, Mark held up his hands. "We forgot something. We forgot to pray."

Others murmured, "Yes. Pray."

A moment later, everyone linked hands. One after another stormed heaven with petitions. The presence of the Lord was so strong, the crowd fell silent, waiting, praying silently. Hope flooded Megan's heart. "Thank you Lord," she prayed. "Thank you." She heard her prayer echoed around the tent.

She also heard a sniff or two as they released each other's hands and moved toward the beach.

Megan started the cart. Mark came to her side. "You're exhausted. I want you to go back to the condo. You need to rest." Peter backed him up.

"Do you really think I could sleep while the boys are out there? No way. I'm coming, too."

"No," Mark said. "I'll not have you put yourself in danger again. When we bring the boys back safely, I want to be sure you're here. Michael needs to know you're safe."

"I..."

"Please." Seeing her stubborn expression, he sighed. "Megan, I believe Michael left because he thought he lost you."

"Oh, no! All right, Mark. I'll stay here, but I won't promise to go to my condo."

His finger traced her cheek bone. "I won't ask more. Thanks."

Rose ran down with the maps and passed them out. The wind ripped one from her hand and blew it down the beach. Bryce ran it down, and handed it back.

As Jay and Mark organized the search, she stared out onto the lake. A dark shadow grew and took shape. Suddenly over the wind, we heard, "Ahoy there. Ahoy. Help...." The wind tore away the rest. "Help...."

Jay hurried toward the edge of the lake. "Looks like someone needs help."

Bryce stared into the darkness. "One boat is towing another. His motor went dead."

Bryce added urgently. "And he looks like he may be swamped."

"The wind is keeping him from coming in," Mark yelled. "We have to help him."

Bryce grabbed his arm. "Come on. My boat can do it." Mark leaped into the sleek cruiser with Bryce already at the controls. A minute later, the boat roared into life and jumped from its berth by the dock.

Dockside the others waited, peering into the darkness...and praying. Some aloud. Some, like her, silently.

"They reached him," someone else called out. Again they waited. Megan's hands gripped the steering wheel of the cart until the knuckles showed white in the light from the spotlight overhead. Another cry. "I think the boat is going down."

"No," said Bryce's dad. "Bryce is there. I can't see, but it looks like Bryce jumped into the boat or is it Mark?"

"Here they come."

A boat took shape close to the dock. A black shape leaped onto the dock and raced toward her. "Midnight. It has to be Mr. McKerne."

The man called out, "Hey. Tie us up. I have a couple of frightened, soaked young men for you."

Leaning over, Bryce lifted the two boys onto the dock, before assisting Mr. McKerne.

With a cry, Mrs. Hanson pushed through the

crowd, followed by her husband and Mark. "Jonathan." Strong arms caught him up.

Mark swung Michael up and hugged him until Megan feared the boy would burst, except he was hugging his dad just as hard. "I was so scared. The boat turned over and we screamed and screamed. I prayed, too, Daddy. Then Midnight saved us."

Jonathan was not to be left out. "He did. He barked and swam right up to us."

Grant explained. "I was just about to give up my fishing after the wind came up, but Midnight wouldn't let me go in. He found the kids."

Mark shook his hand. "Thank you. You were an answer to prayer."

Mr. McKerne appeared uncomfortable with that. "I'm glad I was there. But if not for Bryce and you Mark, we all might have gone down."

Mark stuck out his hand to Bryce. "Thank you Bryce."

Almost reluctantly, Bryce shook it. "It was the least I could do." He looked toward Megan, then away. She understood. From his expression, she thought Mark did too.

Rose stepped up. Raising her voice, she said, "How about everyone coming up to the lodge for hot chocolate?" Laughter broke the tension, and the group found their way up the slope to the lodge.

Michael hid his face against his father's shoulder and cried. "I'm sorry, Daddy. I'm sorry, but I had to find

Miss West. I love her, Daddy." Sucking back his tears, he looked at his father. "I asked her to marry us Daddy. Now she is gone. Doesn't Jesus want me to have a mommy like other little boys."

Megan's heart broke. "Michael," she called softly.

His head snapped around. "Miss West?"

Mark carried him to the cart, and set him down beside her. Michael's arms found her neck, and she got a hug that knocked the breath from her. She didn't care. She returned it in full measure. Tears started down her cheeks. "Michael, you scared us so much. What would we do without you?"

"Daddy. Ask her. Ask her to marry us, please? Quick."

Startled, she glanced at Mark, her cheeks blossoming every shade of red. A grin stretched his lips. "What can I add to that proposal?"

"Mark, don't."

His eyes darkened. "Michael, I guess this isn't the time to talk about this. Miss West has her own life. We can't expect her to feel for us as we do for her."

Megan's eyes widened. "Wait a minute. How do you feel Mark Adrian? You've never told me."

He looked surprised. "I love you. Surely you know that. Don't you?"

Megan shook her head. Michael rolled his eyes. "You have ta tell her so. I did, and she loves me back."

"Is that right?" asked Mark, his gaze on her.

"That's right," she agreed.

"Well, I love you, too, Megan West. I don't want to spend another day without you by her side. I never thought to say this to anyone again, but I love you and...."

Bouncing up and down, Michael interrupted. "Please say you'll marry us."

She gave him a hug. "Oh, Michael."

Mark saw her uncertainty. "Is something wrong?"

"I...I am not whole," she whispered. "My leg. My scars. They're awful. And Jack?"

Carefully, Mark placed his hand on her leg. "Megan. I am marrying you, who you are inside. I don't care about your leg or scars or even if you have a leg. I love you."

His words released her from her bondage. Crying, she flung her arms around his neck and kissed him. "Yes," she murmured. "Yes. I would love to marry you."

The ghosts of Jack faded on the wind. She knew this was right. A certain peace flooded her heart.

Beside her Michael cheered. "We'll be a real family, won't we?"

Mark's smile stretched as wide as that of his son. "You bet, Bud. You bet."

CHAPTER SIXTEEN

...weeping may endure for a night, but joy cometh in the morning. Psalm 30:5b

"It's about time!" Uncle Walfred bellowed above the wind. Holding her aunt on one side against the wind, he pumped Mark's hand with the other.

"Peter thought we'd better see you to your place," Selma said to Megan, her lips near her ear so she didn't have to scream. "He figured you'd rather do that than come to the lodge."

Megan's shoulders slumped as her day came crashing in on her. She'd been too worried to think about her pounding head or her stiff aching leg. She wondered if she would be able to move at all.

Mark frowned. "Megan honey, of course you're exhausted. I should have gotten you and Michael up to the condo immediately. I need to get Michael to take a bath, eat and go to bed."

Michael didn't want to leave her. "Can't I stay with Miss West?"

Mark shook his head. "No, but you can see her

tomorrow. She's not going away again." The wind whipped his hair into his eyes, and he brushed it away.

"That man won't take her away?"

Mark hugged his son. "No, Bud, I don't think Bryce will try to hurt Miss West ever again."

Michael yawned and settled his head on his father's shoulder. His glazed eyes took in Megan. "See you tomorrow. Promise."

"See you tomorrow, Michael," Megan promised, aching now to call him son.

Mark nodded toward her in the cart. "You can run Selma up with you Megan. I assume she is here to help you get to bed."

Uncle Walfred helped Selma into the cart. "Good idea."

Shifting Michael, already half asleep, in his arms, Mark leaned down and brushed a kiss against her lips. "I'll see you tomorrow as well. Dream of me."

Walfred laughed. "I'll be up for you later, my dear."

Megan had gotten the hang of driving the little cart and had little trouble getting it started. Ducking her head, she yelled for Selma to hang on as the wind tried to blow them off the road. Nonetheless, they arrived safely at the condo.

While Selma got off and opened the door, thankfully under the protection of the overhead deck, Megan reached for her make-shift crutch. Her body trembled with weakness and fatigue, and she wondered if she could walk inside even with the crutch. She didn't have too.

Suddenly Mark was at her side. Swooping down, he picked her up, crutch and all, and carried her into the bedroom before setting her down. His thoughtfulness brought tears to her eyes. "Oh Mark. Thank you."

Mark accepted a much more thorough kiss from her. He grinned at Selma who stood in the doorway. "I think I'm going to like looking after someone again."

"But you have Michael."

"Yes, so you'll have two looking out for you."

"Hey Daddy." Michael called down from the deck. "Is she all right?"

"Umm. Confession time. Michael insisted I check on you when he heard the cart."

"Then I should kiss him, not you," she teased, stilling a yawn.

He touched her lips with a gentle finger. "Tomorrow, Love."

Selma couldn't contain her approval as she helped Megan get ready for the night. "Seems like a good man. He loves the Lord and you."

Megan could not keep from grinning. "Yes, he does."

"Michael will be like the child you've wanted."

Megan's eyes widened. "How did you know, Aunt Selma?"

"A woman knows these things. Besides, your uncle and I have been praying for a long time that you would be healed and find a man worthy of you."

"Oh, Aunt Selma. How could you have known? I didn't tell anyone?"

"But God knew, and He had us and, I am sure, others praying for you. Your parents had a pretty good idea of what was going on. They were praying and waiting for you to come to them." Pulling up the covers, she tucked them under Megan's chin like her mother used to do. "When God took them, Wally and I felt the burden to take you as our own. And see," she said with a smile, "how wonderfully God has worked?"

"Thank you, Aunt Selma. Thank you for not giving up on me."

At the door, Selma snapped off the light. "God doesn't," she said softly, then added. "I do believe the wind has died down again." A moment later, Megan heard the front door close.

"Thank you Lord." she murmured, falling to sleep with a smile.

"Tomorrow."

Actually, it was long past noon by the time she awoke, feeling surprisingly refreshed. The burn on her face had eased, and the throbbing in her head had dulled to a distant rattle. She even managed to hobble to the bathroom for a shower, and could take a couple of steps without the crutch.

Her leg still ached, and she stopped to swallow down one of the pills Peter left her with a glass of apple juice. Her rumbling stomach called for something more.

She found her phone in a bed of rice on the counter. Maybe next time, she'd choose one that repelled water a little better. Still, she smiled. Even without the phone God took care of her.

Humming a tune under her breath, she settled her hunger with toast and peanut butter before going to her room to dress for the day, afternoon really.

Her heart sang inside, recalling the night before. "Lord, I didn't dream all that, did I?" She laughed, a happy contented laugh. Pulling on jeans and a blue sweater, she hobbled to the front door and threw it open. With another laugh, she filled her lungs with the fresh air that smelled of green grass and wild flowers, and hummed the song that had so moved her on the way up.

"Go with God. Go with God."

She giggled at the sun and laughed at herself for feeling so like a child, unburdened and free. Why had she carried all that baggage for so many years? Why hadn't she heeded God's tender promise and let him carry her load long ago? Finally, she understood.

Come unto me, all you that labour and are heavy laden, and I will give you rest. Take my yoke upon you, and learn of me; for I am meek and lowly in heart: and you shall find rest unto your souls. For my yoke is easy, and my burden is light.

Light. That is exactly how she felt.

Arms pulled her close, and lips nuzzled her neck. For a moment she tensed, then relaxed as she recognized Mark's chuckle. "Sleeping Beauty has finally decided to join the living."

Turning in his arms, she smiled up into his twinkling eyes. "Sleeping Beauty had some very nice dreams last night."

"Ah." Mark sensed her hesitation. "They weren't dreams, Megan honey. I do love you very much."

Picking her up, he deposited her on the nearby picnic table, sat down next to her and held her close. "When I met you, I was still hurting over Venessa. No, not just the loss of our marriage or of my dream, but hurt that I alienated her from Christ.

"Then you came along and awoke all those longings for a home, for love, and for Michael, the desire for a real mother. You loved us both so unselfishly, it scared me."

Tucking a strand of her hair behind her ear, he continued, "I tried to pull away from the bond I sensed growing between us, but I couldn't. You helped me see God's forgiveness, and, in accepting that, He set me free to love you. And I do."

"Mark...."

"Let me finish." He sucked in a deep breath. "I know Michael and, especially, me. Well, we railroaded you into an answer last night. It wasn't fair to you to force an answer and I want you to know I'll understand if you want to think about it. If you're not ready, if...."

"Mark. Mark. Just answer me this. Do you love me?"

"Yes. Yes. YES!"

"Are you convinced I am God's choice for you?"

"I am."

"So am I. Oh, Mark. I left Nebraska firmly believing I would never marry and never hold a child in my arms." She choked back tears. "But God has given me both. I love you Mark. I don't need more time."

It was a long while before either of them said anything again. When Mark released her, he grinned. "You hair is mussed. Want to fix it before we share our news with the family? Since this is the last day for most of them, they're all down at the tent playing games and talking about last night."

"Michael?"

"He's there too."

Mark drove the cart like a sports car, in a hurry to announce the news. Before they stopped, the Salstrand clan poured out of the tent in congratulations. Running up, Michael jumped onto the back of the cart and gave her a hug that cut off her breath.

"I didn't mean to tell," he said bouncing up and down. "But it wouldn't stay inside."

Bryce, too, came and stood by the cart. "I talked things over with my dad," he said quietly. "I'm going into treatment." This time his gaze met hers. "I will not let anyone else suffer because of my drinking."

"I'm glad, Bryce. But you need more than a program, you need the forgiveness and help only Jesus Christ can give."

Bryce shifted from foot to foot. "I'll think on it,

Cousin. I'll think on it." He smiled then, a real smile. "Congratulations Mark. She's worth having."

"I know," Mark grinned. "Bryce, you will come to our wedding."

"If you'll have me?"

Megan touched his sleeve. "Yes, Bryce. We want you at the wedding."

Michael bounced up and down. Jonathan and Cassie joined him. "Wedding. Wedding. We're all going to a wedding."

Uncle Bob yelled over the noise. "So when is it going to be?"

Mark glanced at Megan. "As soon as I can convinced her to set a date."

Michael cried, "September 10th, that's her birthday."

She blushed at the question on Mark's face. "How about it, Megan? Would that be too soon for you?" He murmured for her alone. "I can't think of a better gift I'd like to give you than me--forever."

Megan's blushed deepened. "I can't think of a gift I'd rather receive."

"Then I'll really be part of the family," Michael griped her hand. "And you'll really be my mother."

"Looks like our next reunion will be a whole lot sooner than the last," roared Uncle Walfred. "It'll be at your wedding."

Megan glanced at Mark who murmured. "And, trust me, it'll be a reunion to remember."

In front of everyone, he kissed her breathless.

As of their own volition the words and phrases came together that she set down in her journal later that night.

> *Lord,*
> *Help me live a life of freedom,*
> *Giving you, Lord Jesus, first place.*
> *Help me glorify you as Savior,*
> *As you fill me with your grace.*
>
> *Help me daily walk with you Lord,*
> *Letting go both pride and ego,*
> *Help me lean in perfect comfort*
> *On the Christ who loves me so.*
>
> *For now I know each step is ordered,*
> *By the One who loves me best,*
> *Thank you, Lord, that finally...*
> *Your lonely child is at rest.*
> *Amen.*

Bio: Carolyn R Scheidies

Carolyn R Scheidies is a wife, proud mother of two, and grandmother of wonderful grandchildren she loves to spoil. Though her writing career is important, it is not more important than her family or her faith.

A graduate from the University of Nebraska at Kearney (UNK) with a degree in journalism, Carolyn's published credits include over two-dozen plus books (with several different publishers including Harlequin and Barbour), several of which have garnered awards. She's written features, program material and more for a variety of publications, has a regular newspaper column, worked as an editor, speaker/teacher and book reviewer. One of her Kearney Hub columns also won her an Amy Writing Award in 2013.

Through the years, Scheidies has spoken to different groups, led workshops, substitute taught in the media dept at UNK for several years and has taught adult enrichment writing classes at Central Community College. She has been interviewed on NTV, KHAS and AFR radio as well as in numerous print and online publications and had a monthly book review segment on NTV when she was a regular book reviewer. http://IDealinHope.com.

Whatever she does, **Carolyn's goal** is to share hope found in Jesus Christ.

Check out the companion book set on Thunder Lake—THUNDERING HEART.

For information on other Scheidies' books check out her web site I DEAL IN HOPE.

http://IDealinHope.com

Thank you.
CRS

www.ingramcontent.com/pod-product-compliance
Lightning Source LLC
Chambersburg PA
CBHW032044240626
47154CB00003B/1067